THE SILVER FOX

The Silver Fox

Barbara Delinsky

OPEN ROAD
INTEGRATED MEDIA
NEW YORK

ISBN: 978-1-5040-9136-7

This edition published in 2024 by Open Road Integrated Media, Inc.
180 Maiden Lane
New York, NY 10038
www.openroadmedia.com

THE SILVER FOX

Chapter 1

The Silver Fox. Justine O'Neill would never, *never* forget the first time she saw him. It was a Thursday afternoon, shortly after two. She had just returned to the office after delivering a luncheon address before members of the Counseling Association of America. The balmy April air had flushed her cheeks in complement to strawberry-blond curls which, buoyed by the weather, framed her face and cascaded in thick waves to her shoulders. In the after-math of her enthusiastic reception by the several hundred professionals gathered at the New York Hilton for their annual meeting, her eyes sparkled a bright emerald-green.

As the brass-rimmed doors of Ivy, Gates and Logan swung shut behind her, she stepped briskly toward the desk of the receptionist. Her hands laden with purse, briefcase, and a thick legal notebook, she smiled in greeting. "Any messages, Angie?"

The receptionist's responding "On your desk, Ms. O'Neill" was met with a passing nod as Justine swept onward, through the open archway and into the maze of halls and offices that comprised the inner workings of the renowned law firm. Her slender legs took her down one corridor and up the next, the rapid beat of her high-heeled pumps silenced by the fine cream-hued carpet. At the door of her own office, however, she came to an abrupt halt. Senses suddenly sharpened, she grew alert. Then, drawn by an inexplicable force, she turned her head to the far end of the corridor.

There, at the entrance to the firm's posh conference room, stood five men. She quickly recognized four of them as her colleagues and dismissed them summarily. It was the fifth man whose silent appeal reached to her, commandeering her attention, capturing her eye and imagination to the momentary exclusion of all else.

He was a striking figure. Taller by inches than the others in the group, an air of distinction set him further apart. He was tanned and vibrant, yet deeply composed and notably relaxed in contrast to the air of keyed-up anticipation exuded by the others. His jaw was firm, his chin smooth, his cheeks leanly planed, his lips set purposefully. The face was that of a man on the near side of forty, a man in his prime enjoying life to the fullest. But, above it all and most enchanting was a crown of the thickest, most vital shock of pure silver hair that Justine had ever seen. Sterling silver. Rich and elegant. Gleaming. And, with a deliberateness that altered the beat of her heart, his dark eyes held hers.

For a brief breath of eternity, time stood still. Engulfed in a wave of sensation wholly new and fathomless, Justine was captivated, hypnotized by the intensity of the man. She felt herself probed to the core, stripped of the protective veneer she had so carefully cultivated over the years. She felt suddenly raw, open, and vulnerable. And, she felt terrified, as though she were a small animal, hunted, cornered, and defenseless.

Following the direction of their guest's attention, four other pairs of eyes turned toward Justine. In that instant the spell was broken. Mustering her badly shaken poise, she nodded politely and forced her head toward her office, intent on fleeing the presence that had so totally galvanized her.

"Justine!" It was the imposing call of Daniel Logan, senior partner and son of the firm's founder. "Justine! Perfect timing! Won't you join us for a moment?"

The question, when issued from the lips of this powerful man, was a politely intoned order. Swallowing the tension that threatened to render her speechless, Justine moved to join the gathering, willing her legs to carry her smoothly, praying that she not trip over her feet before this audience of five. Having so recently been the sole focus of attention of so many more, it was ironic that her pulse should be thudding loudly. But then, that earlier group held no one of the magnetism of this unnamed man. If the verbal order had come from Dan Logan, the visual order was from this tall, silver-haired potentate.

"May I introduce Justine O'Neill." She heard the senior partner take a step toward answering her own first question. "She is one of our newer partners, without a doubt our most attractive." The overtone of sexism hardened Justine, giving her merciful strength to hold her attractive head high. "Her specialty is family law. She's built up quite a practice and a name for herself since she's been with us. Justine"—he turned his shiny-domed countenance toward her as she held her breath expectantly—"I'd like you to meet our newest client, Sloane Harper."

Sloane Harper. A large, sun-bronzed hand stretched toward hers, bringing a disconcerted grin to Justine's already flushed features. For she simply didn't have a hand free to meet his. Juggling the notebook and briefcase for a minute, she blushed more furiously. Then, with a deftness which brooked no protest Sloane removed the heavy notebook and returned her grin, finally enveloping her liberated hand in the warmth of his own.

"Ms. O'Neill. . . ." He cocked his silver head with a refined flair.

"Justine, please."

"Justine, then. It's a pleasure to meet you."

"The pleasure is mine," she answered softly, strangely intimidated and, untypically, wondering what to say as she retrieved her tingling hand. Fortunately, Dan came to her rescue.

"Justine has been an associate with the firm for the past five years. She was made a partner in January." Taking delight in the uncharacteristic, if unintentional, gentleness on display across the features of his young partner, he directed himself to her. "You've just come from a speaking engagement, haven't you, Justine?"

It took every ounce of Justine's willpower to drag her eyes from Sloane's. As though all else had been blocked out by his gaze, she forced herself to face not only Dan but the others in the group. They were all partners in the senior echelon of the firm save one, Richard Logan, the senior partner's son, a new associate fresh from law school.

"That's right." She confirmed Dan's surmise, admiring anew the man's ability to be well informed of his partners' activities in addition to handling his own busy practice. Daniel Logan was on top of everything. *Everything*. In most cases Justine welcomed his interest and insight. Now, however, as she strove to recover from the effect of Sloane Harper's dark eyes as they still studied her, she could only hope that Dan's insight was limited to the legal realm. Her present vulnerability was nonlegal and all woman . . . and a puzzlement, even to her.

"Which group was it today?" The query came from another partner, one Charles Stockburne, a natty, middle-aged man, whose efficiency and expertise brought in the cream of the clientele.

"Today"—she allowed herself to be caught by his subtle note of humor, emphasizing the word as though speaking engagements were an everyday occurrence—"it was the Counseling Association of America. Psychologists, sociologists, counselors, social workers—all hoping that they may never have cause to resort to the likes of *us*," she quipped quietly, though her cheeks dimpled at the tongue-in-cheek barb. Her light laughter was infectious; only Sloane was restrained. Sensing his skepticism and compelled by that same odd force, she ventured to explain. "There are many aspects of their work—child abuse and neglect, for example—in which the law *has* always been viewed as a last resort. It's my job to show these professionals how the courts can simplify things. For years counselors have seen lawyers as the enemy, taking cases out from under their noses and disposing of them with makeshift solutions. It's finally coming to be understood that perhaps the law can pave the way for the counseling profession to make *real* progress."

In the silence that followed, Justine held her breath. Too easily carried away by subjects near and dear, she wondered for a fleeting moment whether she had lost the five with her ardor. It was, finally, Sloane who encouraged her. "Go on." His soft, smooth tone was more than polite; it suggested genuine interest. She was gratified. Even though she had worked twice as hard as any man to gain entrance to this prestigious law firm and much as she respected the legal minds herein, she realized that, in the eyes of many of the partners, she was, very simply, a divorce attorney. Not so in her own eyes. Family law involved far more than the classic divorce. Willingly, she elaborated.

"There are custody issues, even property settlements, which can be resolved in a very satisfactory way by a lawyer who thinks with her heart as well as her law books." The "her" was a slip of the tongue which she made no effort to amend. "The image of the lawyer is, too often, that of a hard-bitten regimentarian. It is our job to try to change that."

"And can you?" Spoken so low that seemingly only she could hear, it was once again as though they were the only two in the hall.

"I hope so." The emerald glitter of her eyes met his dark depths, pulled toward some unenvisioned reckoning. Once more the spell was broken.

"So do I," broke in a harsher voice at her right, that of Joseph Steele—true to his name, hard and dogmatic and a seasoned divorce attorney himself. There had been an undercurrent of resentment toward her from his office since she had arrived at the firm an eager and idealistic law school graduate. At times she had worried that this one voice might stand against her partnership, when it had finally come up for a vote last December. He scoffed at her softness, her sensitivity, her proclivity toward new and untried solutions. He saw her as a rebel. *Rebel, in an establishment law firm!* she had laughed in denial at the time. But mostly he was threatened by the very definite fact that she was a woman, a woman who, in all probability, was a better lawyer than he!

It was Dan who came to her rescue again. "If Justine has her way, she'll have the outside world eating from her hand. She's become the reigning queen of the lecture circuit— organizations, schools, businesses. I'd say she's a colorful asset to the firm!" The twinkle in his eye showed his pleasure as Justine, despite herself, blushed in blatant demonstration of his claim. Thankfully, he took pity on her. "Sloane is the president of CORE International—Combined Resources International. He has just moved his headquarters to New York and has chosen us to represent him. Charlie will be handling most of the work, but others of us may be chipping in from time to time." He glanced at his watch. "How about it, Charlie. Should we get to work? Sloane?"

Justine's gaze followed Dan's to Sloane's face, only to be

caught and held in its charge for a long, final, breathtaking moment before the tall, sterling-crowned man released her to nod his agreement in the direction of the senior partner. Justine promptly took her cue.

"If you gentlemen will excuse me, then . . ." The thick fringe of blond-tipped lashes hooded her eyes as she glanced quickly up at Sloane. "Nice to have met you," she murmured quietly. Then, awaiting no response, she turned and beat a smooth and steady retreat toward her office, congratulating herself on the grace of her exit even as she lowered her head in self-reproach that there should have been any doubt of it. After all, wasn't she Justine O'Neill, attorney at law, newly risen star of the firm of Ivy, Gates and Logan, burning brightly in the courtrooms of New York and at podiums from Boston to Washington? Or so she had been told by patronizing colleagues, and so she indulged in the self-mockery.

Frowning at the irrelevancy of it all, she ran headlong into a figure of whom, up to that point, she had been totally unaware.

"Oh!" Her pale copper curls bobbed as her head flew up, eyes widening in surprise to confront the man lounging in her doorway. Instantly she stepped back. "John! I didn't see you!"

"That much was obvious," he retorted with amusement, noting the momentary dart of her eye back toward the now deserted corridor. "No, he didn't see you walk into me, if that's what's worrying you. Your exit was perfect—classy and polished. That *was* what you intended, wasn't it?"

Sidestepping him to enter her office, Justine ignored his barb. "Were you waiting to see me?" she asked calmly, depositing her purse behind her desk, her briefcase atop it. Suddenly relieved of their burden, her arms and legs felt strangely light and jerky.

John Doucette straightened from his lounging pose against the doorjamb and slowly approached her. "I'm always waiting for you, Justine. Dinner . . . once . . . that's all I ask. . . ." His note of feigned desperation drew no sympathy.

"*Legal*, John. Is there a *legal* matter you want to discuss?"

"It could get down to that, if I'm driven to do something mad for want of you. Come on, Justine. What's the problem?"

The plump leather chair behind her desk yielded gently beneath her weight as Justine sank down into it, kicking her shoes off and tucking her legs comfortably beneath the folds of her skirt. As her eye studied the man before her, she asked herself the same question. John Doucette, her senior by several years, was good-looking in a classical way. His features were all perfect, his dress natty and immaculate. Every strand of his dark hair was combed neatly in place; every button of his dark, three-piece suit was properly buttoned. In his way he was charming and witty—and, in her somewhat jaded eye, totally unexciting. The crux of the matter, however, lay much deeper and entirely within herself. Given her past and her future, she had neither the time nor the desire for any involvement of the type that his often-leering blue eyes suggested. Yes, her reasons were very powerful—and very personal.

With a sigh she repeated her stock excuse. "I like you, John, really I do. But you're my colleague. We're both members of this firm and you know—at least, you *should* know by now—that I won't date someone I have to work with on an everyday basis. Work and play just don't mix." She went through the motion of lifting the handful of pink telephone messages from the edge of her phone in hopes that he would take the hint and leave. To her dismay he merely moved closer, perching on the corner of her desk with the utmost of arrogance. Oh, indeed, she thought, he could be charming and witty when it pleased him. He could also be downright annoying, as instinct told her he was now about to be.

"You'd go out with Harper in a minute, wouldn't you, Justine?"

"Harper?"

"Tch, tch. Ever the innocent. Sloane . . . is that more to the point?"

Her response came too quickly and with slightly too much vigor, belied by the faint crimson tinge which flew to her cheeks. "Whatever *are* you talking about?"

"I saw how he shook you up. It's amazing—the unflappable Justine suddenly flapped. Voices carry quite a way in these hallowed, hollow halls," he teased softly and without anger. "He's a very good-looking man. Very wealthy. Very successful. Very available. And he was very interested in you. . . ."

"John, you're babbling!" she decried firmly, appalled at the extent of her transparency in those few, devastating moments in the corridor. "Haven't you better things to do with your time?"

John would have no part of her diversionary nonchalance. "He's called 'the Silver Fox.' Did you know that?"

"As a matter of fact," she scoffed through thinned and suddenly dry lips, "I didn't."

He nodded smugly, enjoying her discomfort. "That's right. 'The Silver Fox.' And do you know why they call him that?"

"No, John," she sighed loudly, exaggerating the echo, "why *do* they call him that?"

"Because he's sly. A predator. He stalks little things like you and gobbles them up."

The image of herself feeling hopelessly trapped by Sloane's magnetic appeal flitted about her brain. Purposefully she cast it aside. "Aren't you getting carried away with the dramatic? If he's called 'the Silver Fox,' it may be nothing more than a reference to his hair."

"Striking, wasn't it?"

"Yes. In truth it was. It's good to know that one man, at least, has managed to avoid the Grecian Formula habit!"

John patted his own dark hair gingerly. "Now, now, Justine, that's hitting below the belt. People in glass houses—"

"John! That's enough!" She couldn't begin to count the number of times she'd been accused of coloring her hair. But its strawberry-blond shade was rich and natural, a legacy from the father she hadn't seen in over twenty years. Thought of him made her momentarily testy. "What *is* the point of this whole conversation?"

John's eyes flickered mischievously. "Just trying to tell you about the man you may be involved with."

"I *won't* be involved with Sloane Harper!" she countered, again too vehemently, her temper beginning to fray. "He's a corporate client of the firm. From what you yourself say, he needs neither a divorce attorney nor a family law specialist. If I hadn't returned to the office at that particular moment, I wouldn't even have met him." The thought brought with it a gamut of emotional twinges, not the least of which was an eerie sense of premonition.

"But aren't you glad you did?" John drawled slowly, recognizing the very tiny bud deep within that she struggled to ignore. "And, looking as gorgeous as you do . . ."

"John, I had a speaking engagement today. Of course I'd be more dressed up than usual." Her tone was one of exasperation, yet as she looked down at her lightweight wool dress, a gentle blue plaid with a mandarin collar and pleats down the front and back tucked in at her slim waist by an apricot tie that blended miraculously with her coloring, she *was* grateful for the coincidence. John, of course, must never know *that!* "You're really off base with this one," she murmured defensively.

Silence hung strangely heavy in the air as he studied her. "Am

I?" he asked slowly, then straightened and stood. Justine had been momentarily shaken by his pensiveness. As he stepped toward the door, she released her breath, only to catch it on the rebound. John's posture grew simultaneously alert. Halting in his progress, he stood stock-still. There, beyond his dark frame, was Sloane, filling the doorway with his presence.

"Excuse me," he spoke softly. "Am I interrupting anything?" His dark eyes swung from Justine to John, studying the latter for an instant of sizing-up before returning to her. His words suggested a legal conference; the faint twist at the corners of his lips suggested something entirely different.

"No, no, Mr. Harper," John spoke smoothly, extending his hand in introduction. "I'm John Doucette, also of the firm. Justine and I are finished."

The finality of his declaration held far deeper meaning for the two lawyers and would, in future days, come to be recalled by each. Sloane took it at face value, his inner thoughts well hidden behind a benevolent smile.

"I suddenly realized," he began confidently, "that I still had Ms. O'Neill's notebook." To her chagrin she saw that it was true. "I was worried that perhaps she might be needing it this afternoon."

As Sloane advanced into the room, Justine was intensely aware of the smug grin on John's face. Determined to simply retrieve the notebook and amend her lapse, she stood quickly to circle the desk, totally forgetful of the fact that she'd slipped off her leather pumps. The fact was brought painfully home as she stubbed her toe on the steel leg of the desk.

"Aahhh! My God!" She doubled over and grabbed the corner of the desk. Her jaw clenched, she pushed herself back into her chair.

"I'll leave you two now" came John's merry call from the door.

He had seen any number of Justine's minor calamities, and the knowing smile on his face as he saw Sloane circle the desk spoke for itself. Mercifully, he disappeared.

"Are you all right?" Kneeling down beside her chair, Sloane quickly lifted the stockinged foot which her own fingers tried desperately to massage.

"Yes, I'm fine," she murmured in disgust, too intent on relieving the pain to succumb to the mortification she might otherwise have felt. "That was a stupid thing for me to do. I'd forgotten about my shoes."

Her hand was cast aside as long brown fingers probed her silk-sheathed toes gently. "I don't think you broke anything," he decided as he lightly rubbed the offended area. "Do you do this type of thing often?"

Only then did his eyes lift. They were dark and contained a blend of concern and query. Justine felt a melting sensation spiraling through her and swallowed sharply. So John's nonchalance had tipped him off, she rued, then laughed at her characteristic clumsiness.

"I'm the firm's own calamity department—but then, they didn't tell you that, did they?" An eyebrow arched before her, its color a more equivocal mix of gray and black. "No, I didn't think so. Well, you may as well know, since you've just found out anyway." She grinned, poking fun at herself easily. "They call me 'Calamity J' for short. I may know my law, but when it comes to things mechanical—even stationary"—she sent an accusatory glance at the desk leg, now barely visible beyond Sloane's large and hunkered frame—"I'm a complete disaster!"

"Ah, so the lady does have a fault?"

"Just that one."

His presence filled the room, warming her. "Well, that's a relief! We wouldn't want the image to totally crumble!" His teasing was so gentle that she could not imagine offense. "And it *is* good to know that you have at least one weakness, like the rest of us!"

"And yours, Sloane? What might that be?" It was her hope that some knowledge of this man's imperfections might ease the flagrant attraction she felt toward him.

His dark eyes studied her, serving, on the contrary, to enhance the lure. He seemed to be debating, in good humor, the wisdom of any such revelation. Shaking his silver head slowly, he stalled. "No, I don't think I should tell you. . . ."

"Come on! I told you mine. . . ."

"Correction . . . you *showed* me yours. And, if my suspicion is right, you'd rather not have done so."

"No one likes to look like a complete ass!" she jibed in self-reproach.

"You don't look foolish, and you know it. You're human."

"And you? What is it, Sloane—this weakness of yours?"

Again he deliberated, drawing out the wait for what she was sure had to be intended effect. Finally he spoke in a velvet hum. "You won't tell anyone?" She shook her head and furrowed her brow in sign of sincerity. "All right then. And . . . you won't laugh?"

"Sloane . . ." she warned softly.

"I . . . talk in my sleep. . . ."

Having expected something cataclysmic, Justine's shoulders drooped. Lips curling down in dismay, she chided him. "Is that *all*?"

"*All?*" He feigned astonishment. "It's terrible. Entire monologues spilled out in the middle of the night. Trade secrets. Confidential information. Personal brainstorms. Everything! It's terrible!"

"Only if you aren't careful about your bedmate!" she quipped, then instantly wished she hadn't. "I mean," she went on quickly, "if there's just *anybody* around at night . . ." Realizing that she was making things worse, she stilled.

"Precisely."

It was one word, yet the gleam in his eye spoke volumes. Justine bit her lip to stem further blunder. Her toe felt fine now, free of pain yet tingling beneath the hand that continued to hold it. As the seconds passed, the tingling spread upward, through her body, lodging in the knot at her throat. Her eyes linked with his in helpless captivity. Finally, she forced herself to speak.

"My foot is much better. Thank you." At her hint he put the injured appendage gently to the carpet and straightened. If his height had struck her when he stood with the group of lawyers, now it was positively towering. Defensively, she looked down at her desk. "And thank you for returning the notebook. You were right. I *would* have needed it at some point, and I might very well not have realized where it was."

"I doubt that," he breathed softly. "But I'd better be getting back to the conference room. Wouldn't want to keep your friends waiting."

Justine admired the broad sweep of his back as he made for the door with long, leisurely strides. "Thank you again."

He turned briefly, cocked his head, and smiled. "My pleasure." Then he was gone, leaving her at last to a solitude which she needed badly.

But her solitude was limited by the presence of the telephone. As if on cue, a soft buzzer rang and the light on the console lit.

Her tapered finger pressed the appropriate button. "Yes, Angie?"

"Mrs. Connely on 78 for you, Ms. O'Neill."

"Thanks. I'll take it now."

With a flick of her finger Sloane Harper was temporarily

forgotten. "Mrs. Connely? Justine O'Neill, here. What can I do for you?"

A high-pitched voice crackled over the line. "Oh, thank goodness you're in, Ms. O'Neill! I don't know what to do. It all happened so quickly—"

"Slow down, Mrs. Connely. Try to relax. Now, what seems to be the problem?"

"He came in the middle of the night. We must have been sleeping. I didn't hear a thing. I guess he used his own key—"

"I thought you were going to have the locks changed last week?" Justine interrupted, hiding the frustration which suddenly surged through her.

"I was . . . but I didn't get around to it. I was so busy . . . with the children and all . . . that I guess I forgot."

"Forgot?"

Setbacks were part of the game, Justine reminded herself quickly. Clients like this distraught woman expected instantaneous results from their lawyers yet were often not willing to make an effort themselves. Stifling her annoyance, Justine probed further.

"Okay now, tell me what happened. Exactly what did he do?"

"He took everything! My silver. My credit cards. Our bankbooks. Even the fur jacket he gave me last year."

As her client talked, Justine grabbed a pad of paper, cradling the receiver between jaw and shoulder as she quickly jotted down some notes. "Anything else?"

"That's enough! He wasn't supposed to touch a thing until after the preliminary hearing!"

"I know, Mrs. Connely. But this happens all too frequently. We are scheduled for a hearing next Wednesday. Until then, there's not too much we can do about it."

"But, he had no right to steal those things!"

"They do belong to him in part," Justine reminded her softly. "But you're right. He shouldn't have taken anything. Tell me, is anything else missing?"

There was a pause at the other end of the line as the woman tried to think. "I—I think that's everything."

"Jewels?"

"No! Thank heavens those are in the safe deposit box."

"And who has the key?"

The voice was suddenly meeker in a dismal way. "Oh, Lord, *he* does!"

It was a common dilemma for many of Justine's clients, women who, for the bulk of their adult years, had been married and totally dependent on their husbands, even to the extent of possession of the safe deposit box key. Nothing like that would ever, *ever,* happen to her, she had long ago vowed. Cases like the present one only reinforced her determination.

"Look, Mrs. Connely"—she attempted to soothe the woman—"don't let it upset you further. I will make some calls this afternoon and see about a temporary injunction. That will prevent him from removing anything else from the house. In the meantime, we'll just have to wait on reclaiming the other things until the hearing."

"But my credit cards . . . the children need things . . . I have no money . . ."

"Your sister." The lawyer thought quickly. "Can your sister help you out at all until next week?"

With a sigh the other woman reluctantly confirmed the suggestion. "I suppose she could . . . but I hate to ask. It's such a messy situation."

"I know that, Mrs. Connely. But you can assure her that the loan is only temporary. After next week, we should have things straightened out. Sound fair?"

Mrs. Connely's voice reflected her more calmed state. "I guess so."

"Fine, then. I'll give you a call back later when I have something to report. Why don't you call the hardware store right now and see about having those locks changed."

"I will." With a defeated "Thank you" and "Goodbye," Mrs. Connely hung up the phone.

"All alone now?" John Doucette called gallantly from the door as Justine replaced the receiver and continued to make some notes, waving him away with a sweep of her arm. But he was not to be shooed off so quickly. "Did your toe survive that collision?" he asked, reveling in amusement as he sauntered up to her desk.

"I'm busy, John. Go call a client, will you?"

Actually, despite their sparring and John's frequent badgering for a date, the two were good friends. John had been an associate when Justine entered the firm, putting them in the same class. The associates as a group were on the fringe of the firm, commiserating often about petty gripes, consoling each other on minor defeats, celebrating together those hard-fought victories. Justine respected his legal ability, and once she recognized him for the ladies' man he prided himself on being, she found she could enjoy him in reasonable doses. This day's dose, however, was growing oppressive.

"The fox is omniverous and an opportunist, you know," he informed her, as though nothing at all had passed since the demise of their earlier conversation. "He leaps and pinions his victim with his paws. Then his powerful jaw takes over the work."

In a gesture of exasperation Justine lifted the heavy fall of curls from her forehead and held it momentarily atop her head. Her eyes sent a dagger of disgust his way. "Is this absolutely necessary? You really have gone beyond the line of duty. As I recall, you've already warned me on that score."

His grin reflected his pleasure in needling her—and, for once, her seeming lack of immunity. "Just thought I'd make my point a little stronger. If you're determined to get involved with the man—"

"I am determined to get involved with *no one!*" She struck back loudly. "I don't understand why you keep harping on this—" In her frustration she flung her hand from her head down onto her desk, accidentally toppling a pile of books that had rested precariously on its edge. "Damn!" she swore softly, then looked up accusingly as she knelt to retrieve the volumes. "Look what you've made me do!" She turned frustration into humor. "You get me all rattled so that I don't know whether I'm coming or going. You do have a way with women, I can say that much!" Flattery, even of the backhanded sort, always did the male ego wonders, she mused.

"Ah, you finally noticed!" He had come to help her pick up the scattered pile of books, serving himself up meekly for the friendly swat Justine took at his head.

"Hey, you two! What's going on here? I thought this was supposed to be a dignified law firm!"

Richard Logan joined the group, his boyish smile indicating his delight at the break in tradition. On occasion Justine wondered how his more staid father had managed to entice the younger, more adventurous Logan into the firm. This was one of those occasions.

"This man," Justine began, nodding toward the now standing John, "is a menace to society. What he's doing in here is beyond me!"

"And you, Dick," the object of her mini-tirade interjected, "what brings you into this madhouse?"

The smile that lit the young Logan's face bore its share of devilry. "An invitation."

"Great!" John exclaimed humorously. "Where are we going?"

"*You're* not going anywhere. It's Justine. She's been invited to join us for dinner tonight."

Justine cocked her blond head toward John, her eyes green in their merriment. "That's terrific! Where are we going to dine?" *Might as well rub it in for effect,* she thought with a grin, taking revenge on John's earlier smugness.

"That hasn't been decided yet. But the command has been issued. You're not busy, are you?" Richard added as an afterthought.

"I am now. Dinner will be fine." Then a strange and unbidden sense of unease crept into the recesses of her mind. "By the way," she asked with studied nonchalance, "who's 'us'?"

Richard looked from Justine to John and back before answering, confirming in Justine's mind what she had uncannily feared. *Feared.* Though she didn't know why. But fear it she did.

"There will be yours truly, my father, Charlie, and . . . Sloane."

The last name hung in the air for a long moment, before John broke the silence with his conspiratorial whisper. "The Silver Fox." As Justine subconsciously caught her breath, both men turned to stare at her.

Chapter 2

It was a dilemma of the worst order. Not only had she already accepted the dinner invitation carte blanche and with gusto, but she had spent the better part of two separate conversations with John Doucette declaring her immunity to Sloane Harper. Having burned her bridges behind her, there was nothing to do but accept the situation with a practiced, if superficial, grace.

"That's fine, Richard. Please give your father the message and thank him for the invitation. I'll look forward to it." Her eyes bore an emerald steadiness that was almost convincing.

"I'll bet you will," John whispered with a wicked grin as the other left the office. "It should be a very interesting evening. At least you'll be well protected!"

The last thing Justine needed, fresh on this minor setback, was John's continued taunting. Willing herself to calmness, she faced him straight on. "I do have an awful lot to do between now and then, John. If you don't mind, perhaps I could get to it. . . ."

"Not at all." The dark-haired man gave a semblance of a bow, then turned and strode to the door, stopping there for a final shot. "Have fun, Justine . . . and be careful. . . ." The drawl in his voice rankled her. Ignoring it, she lifted the telephone receiver as if to make a call, then replaced it as soon as the doorway stood empty once more.

Absent fingers shifted the telephone messages around in her hand. Her mind was elsewhere. Sloane Harper, she had to admit, was a most attractive man. In truth, she had never been as fascinated by a man before. Unbidden, she recalled John's words, to be haunted, then bewildered by them in turn.

Omnivorous. Sly. A predator. They connoted a man who was hard, shrewd, slightly sinister. Yet the man who had knelt earlier by her side, gently soothing both her stubbed toe and her injured pride, had been anything but hard or sinister. Shrewd, perhaps, if his true motivation was imagined at its worst, but certainly neither hard nor sinister. How ironic, she mused, that she should know nothing more about Sloane Harper than the fact that he talked in his sleep! CORE International was a mystery to her, as was all else about this man whose bold bearing had set her pulse to pounding.

Perhaps it was for the best that she not know much about him. Intuition told her that he might put her vows of independence to a test. But then, she reasoned, arguing against alarm, beyond a well-chaperoned dinner that night, she would probably not see him other than in passing along the corridors of the firm.

A frown marred her gentle features as a new question popped into mind. Why *had* she been invited to join the dinner party? After all, *she* would not be involved with Sloane as a client. Was it simply the fact that she was a woman, the firm's token female? Had she suddenly become a showpiece? Bristling, she recalled Daniel Logan's faintly patronizing remarks back in the hall. To date she had neatly managed to avoid that kind of extra attention. Why should it begin now? To her further chagrin, the fact of its presence, for the first time in the firm, was not as upsetting as it might have been. Could it be that she prized her femininity in the eyes of Sloane Harper?

There was only one solution to her wayward imaginings. Work. There was nothing like a sticky case to remind her that she was, first and foremost, a lawyer. Determinedly she focused her attention on the messages which awaited her. Girardi, at the district attorney's office—Fried, at the Social Welfare Bureau—Tompkins of Tompkins, Tompkins and Riley—Tony O'Neill, at the settlement house—and Theodore Marston. Theodore Marston, attorney at law—and as sticky a divorce situation as she had run into. That would be the one to tackle first, a sure diversion which would require her total attention.

She diligently pushed the buttons on the telephone console, then waited while the secretary put her through. "Mr. Marston? This is Justine O'Neill. I received your message and wanted to get right back to you."

The curt voice on the other end of the line was as firm and sharp-edged as was the man himself. "Ms. O'Neill, thank you for calling. I'm afraid that my client feels the terms you have suggested to be way out of line. I agree."

"That's unfortunate," she stated calmly, having expected just this reaction. It was a basic premise in negotiation to aim far higher than what one actually expected to attain; Justine had done just that. "Exactly what part of the agreement bothers you?"

"Most of it. The money settlement, the division of property, the visitation rights—you name it."

Justine was prepared, tapping on a pad of paper with the tip of her pencil. "Mr. Marston, as far as the money is concerned, your client is a multimillionaire. Certainly this lump sum figure is not out of line, especially considering that the couple was married for twelve years."

"It's too high, nonetheless. With a monthly child support payment to boot! We simply cannot agree to that."

"And why not? The figure we're talking about would be very little to a man of your client's standing."

"He has . . . other obligations . . . business commitments."

"Yes, other obligations." Justine had done her homework, having had the husband of her client thoroughly investigated. "I understand that one of those 'other obligations' is a mistress. Is that true?"

There was a brief silence on the other end of the line as the opposing lawyer recovered from his surprise. He had, obviously, thought this to be a little secret between his client and himself. "How did you ever get that idea?" he called her bluff.

But Justine was crafty enough not to show all her cards at once. "I have my sources. And we have uncovered more about your client that any judge will have to consider, should we finally go to court." Again, silence reigned. Sensing her opening, Justine grasped it. "It might be a good idea, Mr. Marston, if we sat down across the table from one another and discussed these matters. *Then* we can negotiate a further settlement."

She had played her hand to the hilt. Without delay an appointment was set up and the matter temporarily tabled. Justine's strength lay in analyzing her adversary, then using instinct to attain her goal. An in-person conference would give her that opportunity.

A sigh slipped through her lips as she crumbled the pink slip and tossed it into the leather wastebasket behind her. *Leaps, and pinions his victim with his paws.* Helplessly her mind reverted to thoughts of Sloane. But his touch had been so soft, so gentle, she mused, recalling the tingling sensation she'd felt. Catching her breath, she forced her attention back to the phone.

Girardi, at the district attorney's office, was the next order of business. "Mr. Girardi," she began, following the suitable identi-fication, "how is our case shaping up?"

"A little shaky, Justine." Though the law firm, within itself, operated strictly on a first-name basis, she always resented the occasional outside male who presumed such a status as quickly as this one seemed to have done. She could only fight fire with fire.

"I'm not sure I understand, Jim. I thought it was an open-and-shut case of wife beating. Isn't that what the indictment read?"

"Ah, yes, ah, that was what we had originally determined."

"However—" she anticipated him.

"However, there is new evidence that has just arisen. He, ah, claims now that it was self-defense."

"*Self-defense?*" Justine's reaction was instant. "Jim, that woman was black-and-blue for weeks."

"He claims she tried to attack him with a poker."

Justine shook her head slowly, ingesting this new informa-tion. "Do you believe that?"

The assistant district attorney cleared his throat self-consciously. "I'm not sure. You're the one who represented the wife in the divorce. What do you think?"

"I think," she countered strongly, "that it's highly unlikely!"

After a pause, Jim Girardi agreed. "I tend to be on your side. But he still wants to plea bargain. He's hoping for probation."

"That would put him right back on the street, free to do God knows what! I can't see it. His ex-wife is a gentle person. If—and I do mean *if*—she held a poker in her hand, she must have had a very certain fear of the man." Hesitating, she contemplated the next step. "Look, let me speak with Marie and see how she responds to the claim. Then I'll get back to you. Okay?"

"Fine. But make it fast. We can only hold him so long. If he gets a reduction in bail, he'll be on the street anyway."

"I understand." She grimaced. "Let me give her a call and then we'll know more. Talk with you later."

Another pink slip sailed into the basket. Worrying ghost creases into her forehead, Justine jotted a note to herself. She was interrupted when the light on the console flickered. To her relief and pleasure it was the O'Neill who had called earlier, her half brother.

"Tony!" she burst out enthusiastically, responding to the unique place this man held in her heart. "It's been too long. How *are* you?"

"Just fine, Justine. How's the eager beaver doing?"

For the first time that afternoon a truly relaxed smile lit her face. "Not bad, for an establishment lawyer," she poked fun at herself. "Tell me about you—what's happening?"

For several minutes she listened, leaning back in her chair with her stockinged feet propped against the edge of an out-drawn lower drawer as Tony outlined his latest endeavors. Chief social worker at the local settlement house, he had never a dull moment. But he thrived on it—as did she on her own work's excitement. Along with a father, fair skin, and similarly amber hair, this was another of the things they shared.

"Listen, Justine"—Tony grew more sober—"I wanted to thank you for what you did for the Aliandro boy. We're all delighted, now that he's been placed with foster parents."

Gratified, she probed. "It's working out well, then?"

"So far, so good. It's a relief for him not to have to face a pair of battling, drunken parents every day and night."

The case itself had been a rewarding one emotionally for Justine. "Every child should have the right to counsel. I'm glad I could have been of help."

"You're terrific, you know! Any flak from the firm about cases like these?"

"No, no. They know that I insist on handling a certain number of *pro bono* cases. Just because a ten-year-old boy cannot afford to pay a lawyer shouldn't mean that he is denied his rights. That child has a *right* to a healthy home environment!"

"Well, thanks to you, he has one now. We're all in your debt!"

With a blush that her caller could not see, Justine minimized her effort. "It was my pleasure. Call me again soon?"

A mischievous guffaw met her ear. "Are you sure you want that? I always seem to find more work for you."

"That's what I'm here for, Tony. Please, do call!"

"Sure thing, Justine. So long!"

For long moments after hanging up the phone she contemplated the success of that particular case. Although ones such as this which Tony had referred her brought in no money, they were, in some ways, the most satisfying—particularly when the outcome was positive.

Once again the console lit. This time it was Dave Brody. "I've just managed to get tickets for the theater, Justine. A week from Tuesday. Eight o'clock. Can you make it?"

Momentarily buoyed by her conversation with Tony, Justine accepted the invitation with alacrity. "Sure thing! What will we see?"

"The tickets are for *Evita*. Have you been?"

"Nope. Sounds good. The reviews have been fantastic—and even though it's been running for so long, I haven't been. What time should I be ready?"

"If I pick you up at six thirty, we can grab something to eat beforehand. Something light." He emphasized the "light," knowing from experience that this date was not a heavy eater.

Grinning at his perceptivity, she agreed. "Six thirty. I'll be ready and waiting. See you then!"

Dave Brody was a steady friend, a knightly companion. Justine had met him at a party several years before, had been dating him occasionally ever since. A stockbroker by profession, he was an avid culture nut. In his company she had visited many a museum, enjoyed not only the theater but ballet and opera as well. Though her own appreciation was more geared for pure enjoyment Dave's knowledgeable commentary always highlighted their evenings together. And, she mused, turning to gaze out her twenty-first-floor window at the steep wall of concrete and glass across the avenue, he made no demands on her—either sexually, or in terms of further commitment. His presence in her life suited her well!

Involvement with the male of the species in other than the professional or platonic realm simply did not fit into her life plan. There would be no misery for her such as she saw day in and day out through her work. She wanted no part of the hassles of marriage, the bickering about the sharing of responsibilities, the arguments about money matters and career. Above all she wanted none of the heartache she'd known as a child when her parents' marriage had fallen apart. She had suffered enough then to last her a lifetime. Indeed, the avoidance of sexual entanglement seemed a small price to pay for emotional well-being.

As she wiggled her toes over the rim of the open drawer, her thoughts wandered recklessly. A man like Sloane Harper, she decided, would demand things. His air of command would inspire total subservience. She, however, was subservient to no man. Hard work and her own innate intelligence had earned her the respect of the majority of her peers. It was what she wanted and she prized it.

Sloane Harper. The Silver Fox. Was he an opportunist? Silver *was* the color of that magnificent head of hair—but was he indeed the proverbial fox? Strangely disquieting, the question was with her for the afternoon, set aside only occasionally by the demands of one or another of her more immediate legal concerns. It didn't help that John stopped by for a final jab late in the day.

"Remember, kid," he said grinning from the door, "the fox is known for its cunning. . . ."

She said nothing, reluctant to legitimize his warning by dint of response. Her narrowed gaze was sufficient to convey her distaste for his humor. But he slipped away undaunted.

By the time six o'clock rolled around, she felt duly out of sorts. With foresight she had taken a few moments to touch up her makeup and brush through the tangle of her waves. The end result, she decided with a wry grin at the rosy image that faced her in the ladies' room mirror, would certainly pass muster.

But when the tall figure, fresh despite his own long afternoon of meetings and unfairly handsome in his dark gray linen suit, appeared at the entrance to her office, her composure tottered.

"All set?" His deep voice surged across the room to enliven her every sensitive nerve. She looked evasively down at the spread of materials on her desk.

"Just about," she answered, shuffling papers in pretense of neatening the desk top as she stood. "Are the others ready to go?"

His dark eyes held hers with nary a blink. "They've gone ahead in a cab. I've got my car downstairs. We'll meet them at the restaurant."

This unexpected twist sent jitters through her stomach. The fingers that placed several folders in her briefcase trembled almost imperceptibly. "Fine. There, I think I have everything."

"Do you always bring work home to do at night?"

"I always bring something home with me," she said with a smirk, "but it's not necessarily night work." On *this* particular evening she doubted she would get anything accomplished. "Very often I spend an hour *before* work looking over my cases for the day. I'm an early riser anyway, and I'm freshest in the morning."

She sidestepped her desk with care, mindful of her flub that afternoon. Sloane hadn't moved from the door. "You look totally fresh right now. Are dinners with clients part of the normal schedule?"

With a tug she hoisted the shoulder strap of her purse, then lifted the briefcase, only to have it as quickly removed from her fingers when Sloane stepped forward. She released it graciously. "No. This is a surprise. Particularly"—she eyed him cautiously— "since you really aren't *my* client. As a matter of fact, I'm not quite sure *why* Dan suggested I join you all. I know *nothing about* your operation."

Sloane flipped off the lights as they left the office, then moved beside her toward the deserted reception area. "That, my dear, can be easily remedied." It was a perfect Clark Gable imitation, yet uniquely Sloane Harper. Nothing about the man, she mused, smacked of imitation. He was one of a kind—certainly in the profound effect he had on her senses.

Now, as they left Ivy, Gates and Logan behind and stood waiting for the elevator, she was acutely aware of those senses and the messages they conveyed. There was a strength about him as he stood tall, a rough six feet four to her five feet eight, and a dignity in his stance that fell short of arrogance. He was masterful in silence, exuding an aura of self-confidence which challenged her. The faint hint of his morning's dose of after-shave was pleasingly light, as was the warmth which radiated from his lean lines.

"Then, tell me," she began, groping for a diversion from these subtle, sensual messages, "tell me about CORE International."

"From scratch?" he asked, boyishly pleased.

Justine grinned shyly. "From scratch. I am one of the totally ignorant." The arrival of the elevator delayed the story as they stepped inside and began the long downward glide. Alone with this silver-haired man in the plush and polished elevator, Justine was infinitely grateful that an impersonal subject had been chosen.

Sloane began softly, his keen eye following the course of the lights on the elevator panel. "The company began as a small operation twenty years ago. My father was its founder, working out of Atlanta, primarily along the southeastern seaboard. When I joined the company twelve years ago, then took over command three years later, we began to expand."

"Was your training in business?" she asked, unwittingly delving into the man as a person. The elevator stopped at the garage level, and Sloane smoothly guided her toward the spot where his car was parked.

"I have an M.B.A. from the Tuck School at Dartmouth, but most of what I do is intuitive."

Before Justine could question him further, he paused beside a small blue Mazda, dug into a pocket for the keys, then opened the door for her.

"Hmmm," she commented, "I can see why you didn't offer to take the others. Not much room, is there?" The car was a two-seater, well appointed though far from luxurious.

His answering drawl was close by her ear as he leaned in to straighten a seat belt. "Not much."

A quiver snaked its way through her before she was jolted by the slam of the car door beside her. Moments later Sloane let himself into the driver's side, then turned to face her. The garage was dimly lit, casting a halo effect around the silver cap of his head. An angel, she mused, but far from a saint, if his effect on her was intentional.

"It *is* intimate, I suppose," he said softly, smiling.

Justine sought sanity by making light of the definite seductiveness of his tone. "I'll say! It's a good thing you don't have a large family!" Once again she regretted her spontaneity the instant her shocked ears heard her words.

His dark eyes were even darker in the confines of the car, his expression unfathomable. The only thing that was clear was his thorough, ongoing survey of her features, as he one by one traced her sculpted lines, illuminated by the very same light which threw his own face into shadow.

"So you *do* know something about me, then." She could only imagine the eyebrow that arched suspiciously.

"Not really," she countered quickly. "I simply assumed . . ." *Very available,* John had said, though that bit of knowledge and its source would remain her own secret. "I mean, no rings or anything . . ."

"Most men don't wear rings, wedding or otherwise. I notice that you wear none yourself." Moving too quickly for Justine to anticipate him, he took her left hand in his, caressing her slender fingers with a most subtle, nearly imperceptible motion.

Humor was, once more, her chosen out. "The last ring I wore"—she grinned sheepishly—"was a beautiful pearl one that had originally belonged to my grandmother. Unfortunately, a bee stung me on that knuckle. When the whole finger swelled, the ring cut off its circulation."

"Why didn't you take the ring off first?" Sloane frowned at the simplicity of the solution.

"*That* was the operable question at the time. I . . . just . . . didn't think of it. Until it was too late."

"The finger—?" To her dismay, he held hers more tightly.

"Oh, the finger stayed, obviously." She forced a chuckle. "It was the ring which had to go. Cut off. In a doctor's office. By a very efficient little tool. No problem . . . but I haven't worn a ring since."

The smile she had expected from him never came. Rather, he grew more serious. "You *are* the master of disaster, aren't you?" At Justine's guilty shrug he continued pointedly. "But that's avoiding the central issue. Are you married?"

"No."

"Divorced?"

"No."

He paused for a moment, contemplating other possibilities. "Engaged?"

"No."

His gaze narrowed. "Living with—"

"No!" Justine held her breath, a challenge in light of its sudden irregularity. She was cornered once more, helpless in a prison of Sloane's supreme command. In the small car in the dim garage the same potent force reached out to her as had stunned her earlier that day. It was bizarre, yet vital; its identity was unknown. As it threatened to engulf her, she struggled to hold her own.

"I feel as though I'm on the witness stand," she quipped weakly.

"Not the witness stand, Justine," he spoke gently, melting the last of her resistance. "You're in my car—my small car—and I simply want to know where I stand. I may appear to be without scruples when it comes to luring top personnel into my organization, but I've never stolen another man's woman."

An instant's small spark of rebellion flared in her, charging her spontaneous reaction. "I'm *no* man's woman, Sloane. I never have been, and I never will be. I'm my *own* person—it has to be that way." Breathless, she stopped. Even in the dark, his faint smirk bemused her.

"Is that so?" he asked, seemingly delighted. But at what? Was it the gist of her vow that amused him—or the challenge it posed?

As Justine pondered the choice, she felt him lean closer, slowly, subtly. His face was inches above hers, his gaze searching hers in the dimness. For a moment of breathtaking anticipation she thought he would kiss her. And, in that same hypnotic moment, she knew she would not resist. Her pulse gathered speed in its race through her veins, preparing her for an experience that was not to be. For, to her odd disappointment, he straightened.

The soft clearing of his throat was the only hint of any possible emotion on his part. His voice was pure velvet. "The others will be waiting. We wouldn't want them to be worried. . . ."

Throwing a devilish wink her way, he started the car and they were off. It took Justine several long moments to compose herself. Fearful of the silence and, above all, her own burgeoning fantasies, she returned to the original source of her inquiry.

"Exactly what *is* CORE International?"

Sloane smiled as he deftly negotiated the early evening traffic. "That's right. I still haven't enlightened you. CORE International is a think tank operation, much on the idea of the original Rand Corporation."

"Really?" she interjected enthusiastically, pleased to find that she would not be sitting in on a potentially boring discussion of dull business procedures all evening.

"Uh-huh. Our business is research. Our clients extend into every major country, plus a number of smaller ones."

"Your personnel—the ones you unscrupulously steal from other companies—" she began with a smirk, only to be softly but firmly interrupted.

"*Appear* to unscrupulously steal. Please. My reputation tends to get carried away with itself."

The fox, Justine mused—sly and predatory. So that was the source of the appellation, contrary to John Doucette's lewd implication. Now, she needed to know more.

"I'll give you the benefit of the doubt this time. So, who are these . . . employees of CORE International? By profession."

The intermittent honk of nearby horns fell to the side as Sloane elaborated. "There are mathematicians, psychologists, engineers, architects, medical technicians, teachers, administrators—you name it. As the need has arisen, I've hired from practically every field. We span the gamut now, as does our research itself."

"Fascinating . . ." she murmured, turning to gaze out the windshield at the riot of colors on the evening avenues. Dusk fast approached, and with it came the array of neon signs and car lights that blended into artistic chaos in this largest of metropolises. Justine always found the urban nightscape enchanting, one of the things she liked most about New York City. Now, however, it was merely a vivid backdrop for an even more exciting subject. But before she could delve deeper, Sloane's voice stayed her.

"Here we are," he announced, pulling up before The Four Seasons. It took a moment for Justine to recall their purpose.

"The Four Seasons! Aha!" she exclaimed. "We're doing it up big tonight!"

This time the lights of the restaurant clearly revealed that arched brow. "Do I detect a bit of sarcasm?"

"From me?" Innocence, feigned as it was, became her, rounding her eyes and uplifting the corners of her pink-glossed lips appealingly. "I have no complaint. It certainly beats the sandwich I would have had at home."

Sloane's dark eyes studied her closely. He seemed about to say something when the valet opened the door on her side and extended his hand to help her out. With a mischievous grin shot back at her driver, she gracefully exited the car and started toward the entrance of the restaurant. Within moments, Sloane was beside her.

Their arrival had been preceded by that of the other three men, who were already seated and nursing drinks when the maître d' showed the latecomers to the table.

"We were beginning to wonder about you two," Dan Logan burst out good-naturedly. "I half-suspected that Justine might keep you waiting with any number of last minute emergencies." The broad smile he sent her way suggested mere teasing.

It was Sloane who answered the charge. "Oh, no. She was right on time. I'm afraid it was my fault." Only Justine knew the meaning behind the twinkle in his eye. "I . . . took a circuitous route . . . inadvertently. But we did make it . . . and without a . . . calamity along the way." Mercifully, he moved behind to hold her chair for her. It hadn't passed her notice that the two empty seats at the table for five were right next to one another. And there was nothing she could possibly do to alter the situation— not that she wanted to. There was an excitement at the thought of sitting close to Sloane, an excitement which—given the presence of chaperons aplenty—rose, unrestrained, within her.

It was not the first time she had been to The Four Seasons. This time, however, the fine linen tablecloths seemed whiter, the sturdy silver more richly polished, the sparkling china more elaborate. For once, the noise of the other patrons drifted by unnoticed. The realm of her attention did not veer once from her own group.

Amid a variety of well-prepared offerings—lobster, rack of lamb, filet mignon, and prime ribs of beef—the dinner conversation intrigued her, particularly as it concentrated on Sloane, the guest of honor, and his corporate accomplishments.

"I understand you spent time last year in Italy," Charlie Stockburne spoke up. "Were you centered in any particular area?"

Justine put down her fork to look expectantly at Sloane, who had finished and now sat comfortably back in his seat. She noted the faint crinkles of white-on-tan at the corners of his eyes, and wondered how much of his time was spent working in the sun. As she watched, the grooves at the corners of his lips deepened, accentuated by the more serious discussion.

"I did spend several months there. We were hired by a group of citizens—a privately funded restoration group—to study several problems that have been plaguing the government for years."

"Such as . . ." Justine's appetite, sated in the physical sense but barely whetted in the intellectual, brought heightened life to her features.

"Such as the problem of the Leaning Tower," he said, smiling at her, "which threatens to one day topple completely. Such as the matter of moisture in Venice—in terms of endangering both the wealth of art work and the city itself."

She was surprised. "Then you aren't dealing primarily with military issues?"

Sloane's gaze reflected his respect for her insight. "*You* must be familiar with the history of the Rand Corporation. It began as a military-directed operation, then branched out some fifteen years ago. *We* began from the opposite direction. Some of our original projects, particularly once our expansion was underway, dealt with transportation problems, pollution problems, housing problems. They have, perhaps, been our specialty, though we've had our share of military-related contracts."

Once again Sloane monopolized her attention. The how and why were still an enigma. But when he talked, she listened—of her own free will and to the exclusion of everything else. Now, Richard Logan's voice startled her.

"You aren't advocating a buildup of arms in the underdeveloped countries, are you?" he asserted, a pacifist bent in his question to Sloane.

Her strawberry-blond tresses swung round as Justine's eyes flew back to Sloane's. This was the first such challenge of the evening. With a touch of apprehension she awaited his response, wondering exactly how he would handle the issue.

It was nearly imperceptible, that slight up-tilt of his firm chin, but it was a gesture of acceptance, a rising to face the test, just as Justine sensed this tall, broad-shouldered man would always do. He spoke with command and calm assurance.

"Personally, given my choice, I would never advocate a buildup of arms. But, in the first place, I don't always have my choice, and, in the second, my personal opinion has no role in the outcome of our research. I hire experts in every pertinent field. It is their job to face a situation, analyze it in the most thorough possible way, then present the alternatives, along with their own recommendations. No *one* man can ever make a decision in any project."

"But *you* are against military buildup?" the youngest lawyer persisted. A glance across the table could reveal the thinning of his father's lips.

Sloane was undaunted, his eyes now black, rich in conviction. "On principle, I am. If, however, I were a small, newly emergent nation, struggling for survival, and I was surrounded on all sides by significant military might, you can bet I would arm—arm quickly and as powerfully as I could. The name of *that* game is survival."

Justine gasped at the eloquence of his expression. She, too, was against armament, yet she had to agree with Sloane's premise. Lord only knew how hard she had fought for some of *her* cases, those in which she honestly believed that an injustice was being perpetrated. In some instances it *came* close to the survival of her client.

"And I think we're ready for coffee and dessert," interrupted Dan, striving to ease the intensity which now held the group at sharp attention.

Justine passed up dessert, opting for a cup of strong and steaming black coffee instead. Though the talk lingered on less emotional issues, her thoughts focused on the man beside her. She noted his hand, easily toying with the unused fork by his place setting. Dark hairs emphasized its manliness, corded lines its strength. *Paws. The fox pinions his victim with his powerful paws.* What might it be like to be pinioned by those hands? Fingers long and straight, nails well trimmed and buffed, palms large enough to encompass her shoulders completely. Justine wondered if they would, then chided herself for her foolishness. After all, despite the intimacy of that small blue Mazda, Sloane had driven her here as a service. She was a lawyer in the firm which now represented his concerns—that was all. Once again she asked herself why she had been invited along tonight. Ironically, she found that she no longer cared. It was enough that she had the opportunity of learning more about this man. It had been a thoroughly enjoyable experience.

When the group stood to leave, she presumed she'd find a cab outside to return her to her apartment. When Sloane took her hand and tucked it smoothly in the crook of his elbow, she looked up questioningly.

"I can drop Justine off at her place," he announced to the group as a whole, though his downward gaze singled her out.

A warning bell jangled in her brain. "Oh, that won't be necessary. I can very easily take a cab." The eyes of the others were on her; her eyes held Sloane's.

His smiled softly. "It's no problem. After all, your briefcase is still in my car."

The rose flush which lit her cheeks betrayed the fact of her forgetfulness. Her notebook . . . now the briefcase. Would he suspect that she had done it on purpose? Had she . . . subconsciously, of course? She was given no time to consider the possibility, for with leave-taking underway Sloane led her outside, retaining her hand until she was safely stowed in his car once more. Only then did the thudding of her heart pose second thoughts as to the wisdom of this vehicular convenience. But the car moved out into the traffic and she had no out. Softly, she gave her address to the handsome driver, and they were on their way.

Chapter 3

Whereas the drive *to* the restaurant had been filled with talk, the return trip was noticeably devoid of it. A watchful silence filled the air, charging the confines of the small car with a growing anticipation. Justine's senses were alive, aware of every vital aspect of the outwardly relaxed man beside her. Only the pulse of a nerve at his temple told of an inner working that decried total calm.

In profile he was striking. The fullness of that silver-sheened hair fell in casual disregard across the lightly furrowed plane of his brow, leading her very appreciative eye down a straight and character-revealing nose to his mouth, that mouth whose lips could be gentle in smile or staunch in control—as they had been earlier that evening under Richard Logan's pointed questioning.

Justine shifted in her seat, cornering herself against the door to better see him with assumed nonchalance. Her surreptitious glances had become less surreptitious with repetition. Sloane's knowing expression as they sat stopped at a traffic light alerted her to that fact. Self-consciously she combed her fingers through the amber-hued waves at her neck, then ventured to break the silence.

"Now that your headquarters are in New York, are you living here?"

"Uh-huh."

"You've settled in?"

"Just about."

She gave him time to elaborate; when he forfeited, she tried again.

"Do you enjoy it . . . living here, I mean?"

The smile on his face was melancholy in the night light. "I spend so much time traveling that I haven't really come to know New York as home yet."

In the ensuing silence, an ambulance rushed by in vociferous haste. "Hmmm," she murmured, half to herself, "must be *some* emergency."

"I suppose so."

It puzzled her that the conversation had grown so stilted. They had talked easily enough before—but that had been principally in the business realm. Was Sloane adverse to revealing the personal about himself? The matter of sleeptalking belied that bent. Then, as she pondered it, the overall situation grew suddenly clearer. Regardless of the motive on the part of Dan Logan for her presence at dinner, she was, indirectly or not, part of Sloane's business world. Seemingly, he had tired of business obligations for the evening. This last—the driving home of his attorney-once-removed—was a simple courtesy. Beyond that she should expect nothing.

Yet the sense of expectancy that filled the car was not solely in her imagination. Struggling to quell it, she turned to gaze out the side window, in an act of perfect timing. "Oh, we're almost here!" she exclaimed softly. "It's that one over there . . . that's right." Her pointing finger guided Sloane in bringing the car to a halt before the gray stone building, a high-rise apartment house on whose tenth floor she lived.

Determined to avoid further embarrassment, she took a fast inventory of her belongings, clutching the purse and her brief-case as she turned to Sloane. He, however, was already on his way around the car to help her out.

"You don't really need to walk me in. There is a doorman on duty—"

But he took her arm firmly. "Come on. I don't want you going up alone." His smooth intensity startled her, adding to her confusion. Was it business or pleasure? Protectiveness or resentment? She had no way of knowing.

If the car ride had been filled with a strange sense of fore-boding, the ride in the elevator was electric. With each passing floor anticipation mounted, weakening Justine's limbs, sending currents of excitement through her. He stood so very masculine beside her—then looked down and caught the emerald sparkle of her gaze and held it for an instant, before allowing her to lower her eyes in search of her keys.

The moment had arrived. The door of her apartment, stark and white, stood before them.

"Sloane, thank you . . ." she began politely, turning toward him with as much courage as she could muster. The last thing she wanted was to say good-bye.

A low oath filtered through Sloane's slitted lips as he took her purse and briefcase and propped them on the carpet against the wall. His straightening motion brought her eyes up with it. "I haven't waited since this afternoon for a simple thank you, Justine."

His eyes were dark and glittering, his hair set to sparkling by the light high above. Then, all light faded as his head lowered, as his lips sought and unerringly found hers. Their touch was warm and light, firm yet gentle. Justine was startled into immobility by the understated power of it all, unable to grasp the extent of her susceptibility, struggling to reconcile her vow of freedom with the sumptuous invitation to submission before her. It seemed a futile battle, with the odds stacked against her.

He lifted his head for an instant to study her features, then raised his hands to gently cup her face, pushing back the curls at her cheeks as he did so. "Justine . . ." he murmured in warning—and she understood him perfectly. Having read her eyes and her thoughts, Sloane knew her outward passivity to be a denial of the deeper emotion stirring within her.

Her lips parted softly beneath his gaze, their silent invitation met with a smile. "That's better," he crooned against their gentle curves. And he kissed her again. This time, she yielded to him, loosing the emotion as it surged through her. It was desire, in its most basic form.

Her arms crept up the front of his jacket to his neck, then coiled around its strong column to draw her whole body closer to his. She warmed, then quivered as his hands covered her back, caressing gently then lifting, lifting her more firmly against him. Passion ignited beneath the persuasion of his lips, which tasted and explored, then consumed in turn. All reserve was abandoned to his kiss, as Justine reeled amid the headiness of the sensual awakening he caused. When he finally pulled back, she felt the loss.

"That's what I've been waiting for," he whispered, his breath warm against the hair at her temple. "It was worth it."

Any word she might have offered caught in her throat, as the real world rolled in like fog off the sea. Confusion reigned in her sensual mist, a sense of fear in her subconscious. The pale hands at his lapels exerted a slow pressure, as she levered herself away from him. "Sloane, I . . . I . . ."

Mercifully, a strong finger at her lips stilled her stammer. What would she have said? She had no idea!

"Shhh. It was nice, Justine. Let's leave it there." With a low sigh, he stepped back himself. "Have you got your key?"

Regaining a semblance of composure, she dropped it in his upturned palm, then watched him open the door. "Thanks," she murmured, as he returned the key and stood aside to let her pass through.

"Ah . . . Justine. . . ?" His tone was suddenly lighter.

From across the threshold she turned. "Y—yes?"

"Your things. . . ?"

Before her, he held her briefcase and purse. With a sheepish smirk she took them. "I think I'm hopeless," she laughed softly at herself, shaking her light copper curls in despair.

Sloane's hands sought refuge in the depth of his pants' pockets. "Not entirely." The crinkles at his eyes suggested inner laughter. "You're reputed to be a great lawyer, and"—his voice lowered—"you do kiss beautifully." With the warm pop of one thumb against the button of her nose, he strode back down the hall toward the elevator, sparing her the indignity of her rampant blush.

Once safely locked within her apartment, she stood in stunned silence, leaning back against the door, her arms hanging limply by her sides. The racing of her pulse gradually slowed as the tingle of desire subsided. *Desire.* It was an awesome force, she realized, suddenly understanding the fear that lurked in the recesses of her mind. For the first time in her twenty-nine years, desire had overpowered her. What else could have explained the abandon with which she had returned Sloane's kiss? But the far reaches of desire were a mystery still. Where would it take her if she gave it free rein?

Where indeed, she scoffed. Desire would lead to physical involvement and in turn to an emotional quagmire from which she might be unable to free herself. That was what she'd avoided all these years. She wouldn't let history repeat itself. Certainly the forfeit of sensual gratification was well worth her peace of mind.

Pushing away from the door and walking to the sofa to deposit her bags, she turned out of habit to the telephone pad by the refrigerator.

"Everything quiet here, Justine. Am off to work. See you in the morning. Susan."

The notes rarely said more, yet they were always appreciated, as was Susan herself. A nurse, she worked the night shift. It was a perfect setup for them both—sharing the apartment in passing, so to speak. They got along famously, though the time they spent together was limited. At times Justine wished it was greater; now, however, she was glad to be alone.

Changing into a long, white terry robe, she helped herself to a tall glass of iced water, then sank into the sofa. Through it all her thoughts were of Sloane. He had taken her by storm, to say the least. Her defenses had never been crushed as decisively as they had been on this one eventful day. *Day.* She stopped herself in amazement, then corrected herself. *Less than half a day!* And in that less than half a day she'd been shaken to the core by a depth of desire she hadn't known she possessed.

Would she see Sloane again? The chances were good that their paths would cross at the firm. But after hours—would he seek her out? Would there be a repeat of that soul-reaching kiss? A tremor of excitement coursed through her at the memory of it. His hands had cupped her shoulders and drawn her closer—was this the fox pinioning his victim? If so, she was an easy mark, willing prey for the marauder.

A shiver passed through her in reaction to the image. Thank goodness Susan was *not* here, she mused. The utterly vulnerable Justine O'Neill who sat now on the oatmeal-hued upholstery, flushed and warm in the aftermath of passion, was a far cry from that other Justine who so capably and with such dignity could conduct her legal affairs day after day. Oh, Susan Bovary had seen her in a bad time or two, but nothing, she smirked ruefully, could rival her present state of light-headed agitation! "Did you know that the fox does most of his hunting between dusk and dawn?"

"No, John, I didn't. Any other gems you would like to pass on?"

"That's it for now, babe," he said over the interoffice line. "Just thought I'd give you something to think about."

Picturing his smug smile, Justine was grateful that he could not see her expression. It had been a bad morning, and with a minimum of sleep the night before she was not quite up to par in the good-humor department.

"You can't believe how much I appreciate that," she murmured facetiously.

"Ah, ah, sarcasm will get you nowhere. Tough morning, Justine? You sound tired."

"Very perceptive." She pushed aside a scramble of curls to rub her forehead, where the dull pain of a headache had begun to throb. "It's been one of those days I'd like to forget. Court appearances put in last-minute conflict by delays, uncooperative and impatient witnesses, crotchety judges—the list goes on and on. I have every intention"—she smiled at the prospect—"of going home and submerging these weary bones in a very warm and bubbly bath—and staying there until the water turns cold."

John spoke up in a mockery of astonishment. "Justine—I

never took you for the bubble bath type. A quick and efficient shower seems more your style. You surprise me!"

In truth she surprised herself. John's surmise was apt; she *had* always preferred the shower. Tonight, however, would be different. She wanted to feel warm, relaxed, and pampered. She wanted to feel soft and scented. She wanted, she realized with a jolt, to feel feminine.

"It's part of the mystique, my friend. And," she retorted smoothly, "the sooner I get done with this work, the sooner I can get out of here and indulge. *Capiche?*"

"I got ya! Go to it!"

With a sigh she did, but it was tough going from the start, a dire continuation of the morning's frustration. No one she phoned was in and every form she completed lacked some vital bit of information which she could not lay her hands on in the instant. Of the no less than six calls she received in an hour, five involved either complaint or criticism. An evening of pure relaxation had become an absolute necessity by the time she neatened her desk at six thirty.

"So you're still here?"

Justine's head flew up to find none other than the cause of her sleeplessness last night. Sloane hadn't been far from her thoughts all day, an undercurrent of mystery which only served to aggravate her steadily fraying nerves. Now, she steeled herself against his subtle command.

"Just about finished," she spoke brusquely. "It's been an awful day. I'm very happy to see it end."

Sensing his approach, she continued to pack folders into her case as though she were alone.

"That bad?" he asked quietly.

"That bad." One more folder. The Ryder case. *Where was it?*

"Have them often?"

"Not very." Impatient fingers flew to the file cabinet behind the desk, yanked out a drawer, then dug into the *R* 's. Regan. Rollins. Rohmer. Ryan. No Ryder. *Where was it?* Check again. Rollins. Rohmer. Ryan. No Ryder.

"Try S."

"It's Ryder. It doesn't begin with S."

"Look under S anyway."

With a grimace of disgust she flipped to the first *S.* Ryder. An apologetic smile teased her lips as she shook her head, then she lowered her head to rest on the top of the cabinet. "How did you know?"

His voice was much closer. "It's a common mistake in the rush of filing. Last *R*—first *S.* It's done all the time."

Red-blond waves rippled down her back as Justine tilted her head up in supplication. "Why me? Why today?" Then she groaned as she bowed her head again. "I have such a headache." Her soft whisper was muted, self-directed, yet he heard it.

The gentle hand that moved beneath the thick fall of her hair to knead her neck brought instant relief, as did the voice which flowed like a rich and mellow Burgundy wine. "You look exhausted. Just try to relax and we'll get that headache under control. Remember, it's all in the mind."

"Hmmm, a mindache . . ." she played beneath her breath, suddenly giddy.

"No, my dear, a cure for your headache!" Once again the nonimitation, drawled deeply.

It was enough. Eyes closed, she followed his instructions, relaxing beneath his touch until he finally withdrew it.

"Better?" he asked, dark eyes beaming energy into her.

"Ummm, better."

"Ready for dinner?"

"Only if it's light."

"You count calories?"

"Always."

"Never splurge?"

"Nope."

"Never?"

She shook her head, her green eyes locked into the dark and beckoning depths of his.

"*Never?*"

"Well . . ." she relented at last, "*almost* never."

His smile melted the last of her tension like a magic wand, hovering over her, making everything right. To her astonishment, she felt suddenly refreshed.

"Come on, Justine. Let's go. I'm starved." With firm command the large hand closed warmly over hers. Thoughts of an evening of leisurely bathing were fast forgotten.

Dinner was at a small French restaurant in the East Fifties. To Sloane's *escalope de veau provençal,* Justine ordered a lighter *crêpe de mer.* A semisweet Chablis tided them over while the food was cooked to order.

"Do you have family in this area?" she asked, after the departure of the wine steward.

"I will soon. My two brothers are holding down the Atlanta operation until those headquarters are closed. Then they'll be joining me here."

"Two brothers? Also involved in CORE International?" At his nod she prodded. "How did *you* get to be president?"

A lusty laugh brought boyish crinkles to the corners of his eyes. "You're very direct, aren't you?"

Shrugging, she looked down at the soft ruffle of her white blouse. "It's often the fastest way to get information. I'm sorry if I sounded offensive." Sincerity filled her green eyes as she dared to meet his gaze. His amusement puzzled her.

"Please, Justine. Never apologize for expressing yourself freely. I admire your ability to do it. As for your question, it's a legitimate one. I happen to be the oldest of the three of us, with five years over Tom, who's thirty-four, and six over Chad, who will turn thirty-three next month." Justine made the mental calculation, as he must have known she would. That made him thirty-nine. As though anticipating her, he added softly, "My father was totally gray at twenty-eight."

Her utter transparency brought a crimson flush to her cheeks. Hastily she tried to cover her footsteps. "Then it was a matter of seniority—the presidency of CORE International?"

"Not really. I'm better suited for the overall administration of the company than either Tom or Chad."

"No modesty there . . ." she teased pertly.

"Modesty has its proper place. *Facts* are what is important when it comes to running a multimillion-dollar organization." He spoke with patience, soft yet emphatic. "My training and strength is in administration. I have a better overall feel for the organization than do either of my brothers. Their interests are more specialized. Tom is a linguist by profession, Chad an engineer. They are both extraordinarily well trained—I couldn't hold a candle to either of them in his own field! And they would no more venture to take over the general operation of CORE International than I would their individual departments."

Justine could find no fault with his reasoning. It was her own that seemed misguided. "You've never married?" The words had bubbled up from nowhere. Her teeth dug into the softness of her lower lip as she wondered whether he would be offended at *this* forwardness.

He leaned back in his seat, ostensibly comfortable with the question. "No. I've never married."

"May I ask why not?" Though soft-spoken and in her own

voice, Justine wondered what demon tossed out these marginally impertinent questions.

Again Sloane was not fazed. "It's really very simple. I'd never found a woman with whom I cared to spend the rest of my life."

The information settled slowly into her consciousness as she puzzled with his odd choice of verb form. But it was one mystery too many. "That's funny," she said, smiling. "I would have expected to hear some excuse about the demands of your work or the freedom and fun of the bachelor life. Certainly you must date?"

"I do." He nodded, more enigmatically than ever. His expression was unfathomable, his eyes sharp, his silver hair shining, his jaw set firm, and his lips stretched into a half smile. There was a lazy satisfaction about him, a smugness at her curiosity. "Do you?"

Fresh on her attempts to picture the types of women that Sloane Harper might date, Justine was taken off guard. "Ah, yes. On occasion. I really don't have time—" It was her own conscience that stopped her. "Uh . . . strike that!" She grinned in embarrassment, caught in her own trap. "I really don't *make* the time. And there is a definite shortage of men who can accept my terms. . . ."

"So *you* set the terms?"

"Yes." Her eyes were the color of bright emeralds, glittering with personal conviction.

"And what might they be?" He brought both hands together before him, steepling his fingers pensively, confidently.

Held in a stunning visual bondage, Justine experienced a fleeting moment of panic. It was as though anything she might say to this man on this subject would be purely theoretical, for he would have his way in the end. Absurd it was, yet she felt that he somehow controlled her destiny.

"Ah . . ." she stammered uncomfortably, wrenching her mind free, then opting for the truth in what seemed the squaring off in a battle of wills. "I won't become involved . . . deeply involved . . . with any man. I don't want any long range commitments."

"Sounds very cut-and-dried."

"Perhaps."

"Is it your career that's so important to you?"

His look of well-tempered amusement spurred her on. "In part. I want my career, yes. But, even more importantly, I don't want marriage."

"Ah . . . marriage." He exhaled lengthily. "So you're against marriage. Any special reason?"

There were many special reasons, most relating to her experience as a child when her parents' marriage had shattered into a thousand anguished pieces, stinging her badly. But that was in the past. "Nothing more than what I see every day in my work," she said with a shrug, though her features were far from nonchalant.

Sloane averted his eyes to follow the slow motion of his fingers as they twirled the stem of his wineglass. For a long time he said nothing. Then he looked up and challenged her. "Why did you agree to have dinner with me tonight?"

The question was one which stymied even Justine. How *had* it come to pass? She couldn't even recall. There was something about a headache, his hand massaging relaxation back into her, his voice crooning soft orders by her ear. Tingling anew, she smiled and ad-libbed as best she could. "I was in need," she enunciated each word clearly, "of refreshment. . . ."

When Sloane smiled warmly at her, that refreshment was heady. Mercifully, the waiter chose that moment to bring their dinner, and the conversation lightened up.

"That's a nice building you live in. Do you live alone?" he

asked, sampling his veal, tasting it, then smiling in approval of its subtle seasoning.

Justine answered easily. "No. I share the apartment with a friend, Susan Bovary. She's a nurse."

"That's fortunate," he smirked, "if one is accident-prone."

"—as I am? Go on. I dare you. I can take it." She chuckled pertly, then took him off the spot. "Actually, we met in the emergency room of the hospital. I had dropped a large container of orange juice concentrate from the freezer onto the floor—and it landed on my toe. I was barefooted."

Sloane's eyes narrowed. "You've got to be kidding. . . ."

"Don't I wish it." She spoke with due remorse. "It's costing a bundle—all these emergency visits. *That* one required four stitches. The only good thing about it was Susan. She was just going off duty and helped me get back home. When she saw the apartment and the extra room going to waste, she asked if I needed a roommate. That was four years ago. It's worked out well."

Sloane shook his silvered head in disbelief. "You dropped a container of orange juice concentrate on your bare toe. . . . Lord help us!" He lifted his eyes heavenward for a brief moment, then returned to his dinner. "She works the night shift, I take it?"

"Yes. We see each other on weekends, but otherwise it's a short note here or there."

"Very convenient for you . . . if, that is, you want a bedtime companion. . . ." The suggestiveness in his tone brought Justine's head up with a start. *From dusk to dawn,* John had said, *the fox hunts.* Was Sloane hunting now? Foolishly, she had shown him the trump card which had often in the past saved her from an annoying and persistent would-be bedmate. The mention of a roommate was a sure coolant to a man's lust. Now, she didn't even have that excuse. Did she want it?

For an instant, as their eyes held one another's, a current of awareness sizzled between them. In Justine it kindled that very heady spark of desire—a desire that only Sloane appeared to have the knack of fueling. Though she dragged her gaze away, he caught her vulnerability and diplomatically changed the subject, directing the conversation to a safer topic as they finished their dinner. Later, when he drove her home, she found herself intent on prolonging the moment of departure.

In addition to being compellingly attractive, Sloane Harper, she discovered, was as interesting a companion as she had found yet. He may not have had the expertise in music that Dave Brody had or the detailed knowledge of literature that Sam Allen, another of her past beaux, had, but he was, in the all-around sense, a challenge.

"Would you like to come up for a last cup of coffee?" she ventured timidly, but he quickly shook his head.

"No, thanks, Justine. I'll walk you up—I'd like to see the *inside* of your place—but then I've got to be moving along. There's a meeting of the board at nine tomorrow morning. If I'm late, there will be all hell to pay!"

The "inside" of her place, as Sloane had put it, was thankfully neat. "Living room . . . kitchen . . . two bedrooms . . . and a bath." Her slim hand gestured in a slow arc.

"Very nice," he murmured, wandering deeper into the living room to admire the plush shag carpet, the bamboo wall units, the low end tables, and the sectional sofa. "Did you decorate it yourself?"

"Yes. I love doing that type of thing," she offered softly, feeling strangely shy and on display with Sloane here at her own home. Yet she was proud of the decor—a palette of creams and cocoas spiced with splashes of color in artwork and accessories.

"These prints are fascinating." He stood before a triptych

on the far wall—three oversized oils, tall and narrow, which depicted a wilderness scene in the running, from the open freshness of a babbling stream to the more static expanse of a deer-dotted meadow to the dark of the forest. It was this last to which his eye strayed. "It's frightening. I wonder why?" he asked, his question honest and totally devoid of amusement or smugness.

Tucking her hands in the pockets of her gray dirndl-style skirt, Justine came to stand by his side. Her copper curls bobbed as she cocked her head in study. "I'm not quite sure. I keep looking into the trees expecting to see something. But it's never there. It's . . . eerie."

"Do you know the artist?" It was a signed original; his assumption was correct.

"I went to high school with him. We've kept in touch over the years. When I saw this, I knew I had to have it. For some reason, I find it riveting."

Riveting. A powerful word. A word that aptly described her reaction to Sloane. In the instant's recognition, she glanced up to find him studying her closely. Under his inspection her lips felt suddenly dry. Her tongue circled them as she took a breath.

"Are you . . . sure I can't interest you in some coffee? A nightcap?"

His voice was a deep, velvet lure. "No. You'll do just fine all by yourself."

Her mouth opened in protest, then closed with protest unspoken. Time, life, the world—all seemed in suspension as she assimilated the raw desire which filled Sloane's dark gaze. Once again his hair was like a halo; once again Justine knew that his thoughts were far from angelic.

The smoothness of his palm shaped her jaw, his fingers

caressed the softness of her cheek. Her lips parted beneath the gentle nudging of his thumb, which circled them with infinite slowness and devastating effect. Her breath caught and held for one, everlasting moment of expectancy. Then, the telephone rang, shattering the mood with its shrill peal.

"Let it ring," he murmured quietly.

Her eyes darted away from his. "I—I can't . . ." With a move backward, she sidestepped his tall form and made for the kitchen, where the wall phone hung.

"Hello. . . ? Yes, Martha. . . . No, that's all right. . . . What. . . ? Oh, no. . . . Why didn't you wait until *after* you'd checked that out with me. . . ? Of course, I understand . . . No, it just makes things more difficult. After all, we're trying to *negotiate* a settlement, not enforce one. . . ! Look, Martha, since there's nothing I can do tonight, why don't we talk in the morning, after I've had a chance to speak to your husband's attorney. . . ? Fine. . . . Yes, I know, Martha. . . . Good-bye."

Replacing the receiver, she leaned forward, steadying her breathing, assuming herself to be unobserved. When Sloane's lean figure entered her line of sight, she looked up, startled. "I—" she began, only to be cut off by the hands which took her shoulders and hauled her against him, by the lips which clamped down upon hers as though he were taking no further chance of interruption until this particular matter of business had been dealt with.

The dealing was mind-boggling. His initial force gave way to a tenderness which commanded response from Justine as surely as if she had initiated the kiss. After a first moment of shock, she returned everything he gave, then reeled at the havoc of ecstasy his manliness inspired.

Bursts of excitement rippled through her body when his hands began to wander with agonizing precision over every swell and hollow of her supple form. She clung to him, a cast-away, struggling simply to keep her head above water.

"God, Justine," he rasped when he released her mouth to kiss her eyes, her cheeks, the soft lobe of her ear.

The thought of resistance was anathema to her, her vows of abstinence forgotten. In Sloane's hands she was all woman. She'd never felt as sensually aroused in her entire life. The sensations were new and consuming, demanding more and more as they grew stronger.

Beneath her fingers, his muscles tensed. His back was broad and strong, his waist lean in turn. The hardness of his body stirred greater potions through her veins, driving her to sure madness if the coiled tension within were not somehow released.

Slowly Sloane pulled his head up and away, looking down at her, asking the question she asked herself, softly voicing it for eternity. "Justine, should I stay. . . ?"

They had reached the fork in the road, a fork that she had sensed was inevitable from the start. Confusion whipped a ravaged path across her features, slowly, slowly yielding to denial. She'd lived her life based on solid conviction for so long. Now she couldn't possibly ignore those beliefs for one brief brush with pleasure. Her eyes were sad as she shook her head. "Not tonight, Sloane. Not . . . tonight. . . ."

To her total bewilderment a broad smile lit up Sloane's face. "That's good. Very good."

Justine regarded him as though he were deranged. Her nose wrinkled up as she questioned him. "What do you mean—'that's good'? Most men would be furious!"

"But I'm not 'most men' and I don't like the idea of your hopping into bed with a man—any man—you've only known for little over a day." His grin was brilliant. "You may be a very passionate red-headed vixen, but you have restored my faith in the morality of women!"

A slow anger began to rise, overshadowing the desire which had moments earlier captivated Justine. "You tested me."

"You might say that."

With a vigorous shove, she pushed him away and stormed into the living room. "I think you'd better leave now," she called loudly over her shoulder, pacing to the fireplace and planting herself there, arms crossed over her chest, with her back to the room. She didn't hear his approach, merely felt the warm length of his arm slip around her middle and fit snugly beneath her breasts as he drew her back against him once more. Dismay filled her at the involuntary swell of her breasts, the instinctive trembling of her insides. Yet she couldn't get herself to pull away.

"Don't be angry," he crooned against her curls, his body long against her. "I would have been glad to stay. God only knows I'll have enough trouble trying to sleep. But there's more to life than lust, isn't there?" He paused, then squeezed her. "Well, isn't there? Would you rather I was a forceful rogue, taking whatever I could get, then walking out? Hmmmm?"

She shook her head in misery, racked by a mix of frustration and mortification. Of course, he was right! Her resentment was uncalled-for.

"There," he declared softly. "One other thing we agree on. And, when the time is right, we'll agree on everything." His emphasis on the last word startled her even more than his expression of the entire thought. *He* implied a future to their relationship—*she* had not gone that far. "Now." He loosened his hold and turned her around, keeping her well within the circle of his arms. She had to tilt her head up to face him, yet his height was strangely comforting. His nearness sharpened her senses anew, thrilling her with its aura of masculinity. "I have to go home to Atlanta for the weekend—to see my parents and tie up a few loose ends. From there I'm off to Tucson for a week or so—a small matter regarding an irrigation proposal. Shall I see you when I get back?"

Justine was surprised at the question, given his tone of total self-assurance. Reluctant to give him the satisfaction of an eager acceptance of his very open-ended suggestion, she shrugged, feigning indifference. "Perhaps." The feel of his thighs, muscled and strong, lingered as he stepped away.

"You'll wait for me?"

"'Wait'?"

There was a devilish slant to the upward lift of his eyebrow. "You won't go and take up with the first man who comes along?"

"Don't be absurd—is this another one of your little tests?" She followed his progress to the door through eyes narrowed in suspicion.

His laugh was hearty. "Could be, Justine. Could be." Then he sobered. "Good night. And, Justine?" The door was open by his hand; his eyes captured her. "Take care of yourself, will you?"

Unable to muster a response amid the eddy of emotion, she could only look on in astonishment as he reinforced the request with a visual command, then closed the door quietly behind him.

Justine sighed her bewilderment. "Good night, Sloane," she whispered at last into the silence.

Chapter 4

Fate, however, conspired to keep Sloane out of the state for nearly three weeks, giving Justine ample time for soul-searching. Where, precisely, was their apparently mutual attraction to lead? No man had ever inspired such thoughts in her; in the past, there had always been a definite cutoff point beyond which she had simply refused to go. As she had told Sloane, she set her terms and stood by them. Now, however, she found herself rethinking those terms. If she had been drawn inexorably toward Sloane in person, his magnetism in absentia was no less awesome. He was ever on her mind.

One by one she set up obstacles against the possibility of involvement with him; one by one they crumbled. He was a client and, as such, off limits romantically—yet he wasn't *her* client, thereby lifting that professional restriction. He was a man of the world with, perhaps, a woman in every port—yet he was, by all indications, available and interested in Justine. He was a traveler by choice, off and away as he was right now—yet his home was New York, her own for the past eight years.

In the end one thing was crystal clear. Though the power he wielded over her senses threatened long-standing principles which had shaped her life, she could no more reject his suit, should he choose to pursue it, than she could deny the passion he had awakened within her. She was a woman. Never before had she realized that simple truth so clearly.

As the days passed and the rain-spattered streets of April dried beneath the warm May sun, she was mercifully busy. Her practice seemed to blossom in harmony with those other buds of spring—the lime-hued maples over-hanging Fifth Avenue, the pale pink dogwoods in Central Park, the red-knobbed geraniums in their streetside window boxes.

There were clients aplenty and their related court appearances. There were in-office conferences, on-location conferences, and conferences over lunch. There were lectures to plan, research, and deliver. And, there was a victory to celebrate.

"Congratulations, Justine!" exclaimed her friend and fellow law school graduate Sheila, hugging Justine warmly as she arrived, nearly breathless, at the Russian Tea Room for their monthly gastronomical adventure.

Tall and willowy Andrea joined in buoyantly, "We knew you could do it!"

"Another small step for womankind!" The last was from Liz, blond-haired, freckle-faced Liz, and was delivered with a clenched fist in the air, as the four young women settled down at their appointed table.

"That was quite an alimony award—based on *back wages,* no less!" Sheila bubbled. "The idea that a woman has a right to collect for services rendered over the years of marriage is brilliant—particularly in this case, where the husband was holding out on her all those years! Imagine—keeping his wife in the dark about a million dollars' worth of investments—and splurging the profits behind her back! I'm green with envy at the ingenuity of your argument!"

Justine's modesty brought a look of near guilt to her face.

"Come on, Sheila. It was no more ingenious than some of those real estate contracts you've negotiated. Perhaps more dramatic—"

"What's *really* amazing," Liz interjected with obvious pleasure, "is that you've finally gone in for the dramatic at this late stage, Justine. When we were at Sarah Lawrence, you were the most conservative of the three of us!" She and Andrea laughed in easy conspiracy.

Justine had roomed with Liz and Andrea during her last two years of college; she had met Sheila at Columbia Law, where they had become close friends. The foursome met once a month to treat themselves to dinner at a preselected restaurant. Over the years they had sampled the exotic and the simple, the foreign and the American, the outstanding and the mediocre of New York's myriad of offerings. Some, such as the Russian Tea Room, they returned to repeatedly.

"You're right about that, Liz. I *was* pretty conservative," Justine admitted with a smile. "As I recall, I studied all the time. *Period.* I must have been pret—ty bo—ring. . . ." She drew the last words out in singsong fashion, evincing laughing agreement from the others.

It was Andrea, however innocently, who expressed the poignant truth. "Well, you're certainly making up for it now!"

Indeed, she *was* making up for lost time, if all her wayward thoughts were to be counted. For Sloane had become a fixture in those thoughts, the symbol of a sensual excitement she had never known before. She thought of him constantly.

When at work in her office, one eye was alert to any movement at the door, half-expecting him to magically pop up there. When at home, she looked to the phone—hoping, waiting, suffering with each false alarm. The spring-bright streets of New York took on an even gayer glow through the rose-colored glasses of her mind's romanticism. And, at night—at home, alone, tossing in bed, restless and strangely unfulfilled—she thought of him, wishing him back, imagining his presence, fantasizing with abandon and delight.

Given the prolonged length of his absence, Justine might very well have begun to suspect the excitement to be all in her own imagination—had it not been for intermittent reminders Sloane himself sent. At the end of the first week there was a bright red tin Band-Aid box, filled to the top with jelly beans and wrapped around with a gay red-and-white checked ribbon. It had been delivered to the office and bore a note that was short but sweet as were its contents.

"Cravings are something else entirely. Remember, one a day . . . Sloane."

. . . Keeps the doctor away, she thought grinning, following his line of thought easily. But cravings . . . yes, they *were* another matter entirely. And though she would certainly enjoy every one of the jelly beans he sent, her immediate craving was not for sweets!

Then there was the bottle of vintage Chablis just before the start of the second weekend. "To share with Susan, and Susan *only*. My thoughts are with you. Sloane." It was a lovely gesture, she mused, hugging the bottle to her. A sad substitute, however, for the real, live, tall and silver-haired man!

With no idea as to when he would return, Justine grew uneasy. *Had* her interest been misplaced? Then came the rose. A single, brandy-tinted blossom, its shade matched her hair to perfection. "A breath of springtime. Mine will have to wait until I see you again. Sloane."

Mercifully, the flower had been delivered to her apartment. It was Sunday, more than two weeks since she'd seen him last. Tears welled in her eyes at the thought—*his* thought—and she made no effort to contain their flow. Since Susan knew about Sloane, there was nothing to hide. At work, however, tears might have been a distinct problem. There were clients to control and colleagues to confront. There was an image of distinction and efficiency to uphold. And, of course, there were the sharp, sharp eyes of one John Doucette to dodge.

"He's on the prowl, moving in, isn't he, Justine?" At that moment, John's blue eyes focused on the tin of jelly beans atop her desk.

"*He* happens to be a very respectful man—and knows when to *leave a woman alone.*" Her hint sailed right over the head of her persistent colleague, yet her smug smile was duly noted. From Justine's point of view, it made no sense to continue to deny—either to herself or to others—the presence of a special kind of awareness between Sloane and herself. She volunteered no information, however, forcing John, in this case, to either ask his questions directly or draw his own conclusions.

"I checked in my little manual," he began factually, "and discovered several interesting points."

"What manual?" She looked up from her paperwork long enough to betray her interest.

"I was into hunting at one point there. Several of my friends and I used to spend weekends in season hunting upstate. The fox is an intriguing animal."

Justine leaned back to listen with enjoyment to his latest. "Is that so?" she drawled comfortably.

"Uh-huh. For instance, he maintains territorial exclusivity; he claims an area as his own, then keeps all other foxes off the premises. However, he has been known to travel long distances in search of prey. Where did you say Sloane was?"

The aptness of John's analogy brought a knowing grin to her lips. "I didn't—but he is, I believe, in Arizona."

"Yes, I would call that a long distance from here."

"What else?" Despite her initial resistance, Justine now found great amusement in his chatter.

"Ah, let me see. His keenest sense is that of smell, and"—he feigned concentration—"the female fox is called his vixen."

Vixen. Hadn't Sloane himself called her that? Could it be that he was aware of the appellation which his thick, silver thatch inspired? Was he subtly mocking it—or her?

"Justine . . . Justine . . . are you still here?" John's voice called her from her reverie.

"Y—yes. I was just . . . thinking about something else. . . ." she fibbed, frowning, then forcing herself to brighten up once more. "Sorry, I just remembered a call I was supposed to make."

This time John did take the hint, taking his leave of her with a salute. Alone once more she lapsed into deep thought on this most perplexing, most exhilarating topic. But her thoughts had nowhere else to go. If it was the nature of her relationship with Sloane Harper which puzzled her, only his return would straighten things out.

The fifteenth of May came and went with no sign of Sloane. It was four days after that, on Thursday morning, when she least expected it, that she finally saw him. Court had just adjourned for a lunch recess. Justine stood at the plaintiffs table, gathered her papers together, and deposited them in her briefcase, then lent a cursory glance toward her navy linen skirt and beige cotton blouse, both tailored to skim her slender lines and brought together as a set by the lightweight woven vest of blues, creams, and browns which swung freely to the top of her hips. She had chosen her outfit for the day with great care. This particular case, a custody hearing with the opposing attorney a distinctly macho man, called for a certain degree of femininity—enough to cleverly understate the force of the attorney-in-skirts, who might then be able to creep in even closer before lunging. Perhaps, she laughed to herself, there was a bit of the fox in everyone.

Turning, she made her way to the courtroom door then looked up and froze. Sloane stood there, tall and straight, striking in a dark gray suit and crisp white shirt, his silver hair falling gently across his forehead. His eyes sparkled, yet the lines around his mouth spoke of fatigue.

The last of the other people stepped past her and left the room before Justine could find the strength to speak. It had been a long three weeks of wild imaginings, all of which might very well be strewn to the winds of farce within the next few moments.

It was finally Sloane who moved, slowly approaching her as his eyes held hers with the command she remembered from that very first day. "Is there somewhere we can go for a minute?" he murmured softly, his expression held in taut and puzzling control.

Her heart hovered in her throat. "Uh, yes. A conference room. Down the hall." Without further word she led him there, dying a bit with each footstep. The waiting had been frustrating but so lovely—thinking that the end would be pure rapture. Was *this* what it had come to? Strangers?

The room she led him to was small and drab, a far cry from the plush and spacious conference room at Ivy, Gates and Logan. Barred windows conspired to keep the beauty of spring-time on the far outside. Even the spartan table and chairs held a somberness. As she turned to face him, Sloane closed the door. For a breath-stopping moment he studied her, searching her face for something known only to him. Then, he smiled in what she could only term sheer relief.

"Come over here." He cocked his head jauntily and held out

his arms. It was all the invitation she needed. Smooth steps brought her into the embrace which her own arms slid inside his jacket to complete. It was all here—the warmth and the caring she feared she might have imagined. Words were unnecessary. There was only the tightening of his arms as she was crushed fiercely against him, full witness to the thunderous beat of his heart.

She could have stood this way forever, had it not been for the flame of desire which would not stay banked for long. His hold of her slackened just enough to permit the upward tilt of her face. Then he kissed her. His lips closed hungrily over hers, satisfying that initial need before growing more measured. She welcomed his tongue with the seductive thrust of her own, abandoning herself to the spiraling rise of passion.

Totally breathless, she was finally released when Sloane held her back to bathe her features in the light of his gaze. "You look wonderful!" he exclaimed softly and with obvious bias.

A wavering line of worry broke beneath the copper curls on her forehead. "*You* look tired. Was it a bad trip?"

"It was much, much too long. Knowing *you* were *here* was as much an agony as it was a solace!"

She dropped her head into the fitted crook beneath his jaw, inhaling deeply of the scent that was uniquely male—uniquely Sloane. "It's been such a long time," she whispered, closing her eyes and savoring the moment with every bit of appreciation that the wait had inspired. "I missed you."

A low groan slipped from Sloane's lips the instant before he tightened his arms about her, pressing her closely against his length. "There was a problem in Atlanta," he explained with sucked-in breath, as though he had to force himself to talk of business or lose total control of his senses. "I was in Arizona for no more than two hours when I had to turn around and fly back. Then, when I finally managed to examine the Tucson project, there were unexpected problems. At some points, I wondered just when I *would* be able to get back."

"I received the gifts, Sloane"—she looked up at him—"the candy, the wine, and the rose. Thank you. They helped me along the way there."

"They were the least I could do. I didn't dare call . . ."

The reasoning behind that last seemed totally irrelevant now. Justine could only revel in the delight of his return. "Are you back for a while?"

"I hope so." He nodded emphatically, his dark eyes searing her intently.

"Hey, what—oh, excuse me, Ms. O'Neill!" The voice at the door brought both faces around in a flash. Justine instantly recognized the court officer, who had unwittingly walked into her own private and uncharacteristically intimate conference. Sloane let her go, stepping back with amusement at her struggle to regain her composure.

"That's—ah—perfectly all right." She blushed, smoothing an imaginary wrinkle from her skirt. "Was there some problem, Sergeant?"

"No, ma'am," the short and stocky man replied with a wry smile. "Just wanted to find a free room for a meeting. I'll keep looking—"

"Please, Sergeant," Sloane spoke up deeply, "be our guest." He gestured toward the table with his hand. "Ms. O'Neill and I have to be leaving."

"Must you go?" she asked softly when they reached the hall. Sloane took her elbow and began to walk slowly.

"My plane landed just about an hour ago. I came straight from the airport. I still have to stop at the office—and face whatever goodies may have piled up there during my absence."

He paused, turning her toward him again. "Are you free for dinner?"

Justine grinned coyly. "I think I can manage to be."

"Eight o'clock?"

"Fine."

His soft-murmured "See you then" was punctuated by a firm squeeze of her arm an instant before he turned and walked down the hall, then rounded the corner toward the elevator. Had Justine not been in this place at this time for the very serious business of justice, she would have stood on the nearest bench, spread her arms wide and up, and let loose the most earth-shattering cry of exhilaration imaginable. Was this really the sedate and poised Justine O'Neill, who now battled to control such irresponsible impulses? A grin curved her lips as she hugged herself in excitement, then headed for the cafeteria and a lunch she somehow knew she would barely touch.

Her light-headedness carried her through the afternoon's court session, back to the office, then home at last. She was ready and waiting when Sloane buzzed from the lobby. With a final glance at her flushed image in the mirror, she headed for the door. Her outfit was new, one she had bought on impulse the week before. The evening pants were of fine black silk, gathered in at the waist and ankle, fuller in between. She wore a white blouse of matching style, with a fullness at arms and bodice tucked in neatly at the wrists, neck, and waist. Her cummerbund was of pale pink, her shoes open sandals of black patent leather. For the sake of comfort, she had caught her curls up in bright gold clasps above either ear, leaving only a few wispy tendrils to brush her cheeks. *And*, recalling the fox's keen sense of smell, she had quite deliberately dabbed her pulsepoints with Flora Danica.

Sloane was instantly appreciative of the pains she had taken to look her most attractive for him. His smile was white and gleaming, his eyes, devouring every one of her five feet eight inches before he finally breathed a husky "hello." As ever, he was devastatingly handsome himself, dressed in an immaculately tailored linen suit of navy blue, a white shirt, and a dark maroon and navy rep tie.

"Hello, yourself." She smiled self-consciously. Then, she caught a strange twinkle in his eye and frowned in puzzlement.

"Unfortunately . . . not exactly . . . myself," he murmured with an air of mild guilt as he glanced down the hall. Leaning just beyond her threshold, Justine watched the approach of two other men, both tall as was Sloane, and each with a definite similarity of feature.

"Tom and Chad . . ." she whispered in a moment of intuitive realization.

Sloane had time only for a wry-spoken, "How *could* you guess," before the others reached her door.

"Sorry, brother," the darker of the two began, "but the doorman showed up sooner than we expected."

It was the blond-haired one, the youngest of the three, who offered his hand in introduction. "I'm Chad, Justine. You have no idea what a pleasure it is to meet you!" Justine had taken several steps back into her apartment and the two followed her, leaving Sloane to watch with amusement from the door. "This is my brother, Tom." Chad gestured toward the other. "And, you have met Sloane, I believe."

Justine sent a helpless plea toward the door as she laughed spontaneously. "You believe correctly. I'm pleased to meet both of you. When did you arrive?"

"Didn't Sloane tell you?" Tom asked, more soft-spoken and gentle by nature than the others. "We fixed it so that his plane returned from Tucson via Atlanta—we needed a lift, since he was the one who arranged this move in the first place." To Justine's relief there was no hint of resentment—only good-humored ribbing.

It was but a sampling of what she was in for for the evening. Sloane had declared that, in honor of his brothers' arrival in New York, only the best would do. They dined in luxury at La Côte Basque, where she quickly learned that these were not two inexperienced young men seeing the big city for the first time. Both spoke fluent French, as they readily proceeded to demonstrate to the delight of the waiter and the maître d', and each had a thorough knowledge of fine wines and superb French dishes.

"We've all spent time abroad," Sloane explained at a point when the brothers were engaged in intent discussion of the exquisite stretch of muraled wall. "My parents believed in every aspect of education—not only formal schooling but the less formal experiences of visiting different places, different countries, and living with different degrees of comfort. Our own home is on the near side of luxury, but we've each spent time roughing it in the wilds. I spent several summers as a canoe guide in upper Minnesota—it's deserted country up there!"

"I believe it," she answered with barely concealed admiration. "Obviously, your brothers have been to New York before."

"Many times." He grinned. "But this is the first time they're attempting to *live* here."

"Have you got an apartment?" she asked of Chad, whose attention had come back to rest with them.

The apologetic look this youngest brother cast toward Sloane did not escape her. "I'm afraid we'll be shacking up with Sloane until we find something."

"You've got the whole weekend to look," Sloane informed him, indulgent yet firm, "and then I want you *out!* I've lived alone for too many years to be suddenly sharing a place with two guys. Besides"—he grinned at Tom—"you had no trouble arranging for that cute little BMW to be here waiting for you. An apartment shouldn't be too difficult for you to manage."

"Enough! Enough!" Tom's mocking desperation stilled the humor-filled diatribe. "We get the point! So you're really going to take off for the weekend . . . desert us in our hour of need?"

Justine looked from Tom to Sloane, holding the latter's gaze questioningly. When a large hand sidled over hers beneath cover of the tablecloth and proceeded to squeeze it reassuringly, she understood that Sloane would explain later. When that same hand continued to hold hers, "later" took on other connotations, each of which sent ripples of excitement through her.

"Later" was, unfortunately, a relatively public affair—a few moments of slow dancing in the dim light of a lounge at the Plaza while Chad and Tom nursed nightcaps at the bar. "Sorry, Justine, but this is the best I could do for tonight," he apologized softly, as he held her close and rocked her to the sweet sound of a melancholy keyboard. But the music was incidental to her enjoyment. What pleased her most was the strength of the long, lean body against which he held her firmly, the caressive warmth of his voice as he sought to explain.

"I had expected to have been back for at least a week before they arrived. With the delay between Atlanta and Tucson, things got pretty messed up. Mmmmmm, do you smell good!" he interrupted his thought endearingly, then went on. "My brothers can be overpowering when they get going as a twosome."

"You're all very close," she commented appreciatively. "I envy you that." His hand pressed hers against the lapel of his jacket, flattening it against his heart. His fresh-shaven cheek was smooth and snug by her temple.

"You have no sisters or brothers?"

It was no simple question. Tony was her half brother, born

out of wedlock to her father's mistress when Justine was six. As a child she had never even known of Tony's existence. In a way, therefore, she spoke the truth. "I grew up an only child. One of a kind, so to speak," she quipped, though she regretted the evasion. Once having discovered and accepted each other, Tony and she had grown close, in spite of the fact that she and her father had never been reconciled.

"One of a kind? I'll second that! Listen, about this weekend..." She drew back to look at him, pulse racing wildly. "...Tomorrow I'll be passing papers on a home in Westport. Would you like to take a ride up? It's empty and unfurnished and I'll have to pick up a few things to make it livable. But I do have a couple of sleeping bags ... just in case it gets cool...."

As the darkness of his eyes reached out to swallow her up, Justine knew what her answer would be. It was in the smile which mirrored his, in the heart which thudded loudly, in the knees that threatened collapse, in the veins which pulsed desire. "I'd love that, Sloane," she whispered softly, then felt him relax as he pulled her back against him.

"There seems to be so little time..."

Had *he* spoken, or had *she* imagined it? His words expressed the urgency that his leisurely dance belied. It was as though he knew something she did not ... and it frightened her. Had she let herself in for more than she could handle? *No*, she decided with conviction. For the first time in her life she had found something worth the risk of entanglement, something powerful enough to merit splurging on. But her eyes were open. She knew what to expect. And she wanted more than anything to spend the weekend with Sloane Harper at his new home in Westport.

Chapter 5

As she had promised, Justine left work early on Friday, a simple matter considering her lack both of pressing appointments and of powers of concentration. As he had promised, Sloane picked her up at five. She was waiting eagerly.

"It may take us a little longer at this hour," he warned, stowing her small overnight bag in the back of his Mazda, "but I'd better discover just *how* long before it becomes a regular thing."

"Are you planning to give up your place in the city and live full time in Westport?"

He shook his head as he stowed *her* safely in the passenger's seat, then trotted around to slide behind the wheel. "I'll keep the apartment for use when I need to stay in the city. If I have either very early or very late meetings, it might come in handy. Or, I may want to loan it to a visiting client."

Justine nodded her understanding and agreement, though her thoughts had already begun to wander. "You look great . . . in jeans," she blurted out on impulse. "I've only seen you wearing a suit."

Great was an understatement. When Sloane paused to grin at her before starting the car, she realized to what extent. He was masculinity personified, from the corded stretch of broad shoulders beneath the khaki cotton twill of his shirt to the lean-ness of his denim-hugged hips. In motion, his lines were fluid; at rest, as they were now, he exuded strength and assurance.

"You don't look bad yourself," he countered, underscoring his words with a thorough perusal of her slender length. She also had worn jeans, topped by a light blue turtleneck of a loose cotton knit, with a change of more seasonal clothes in her bag. Despite the thorough covering of her every curve, she felt suddenly naked. Flags of pink waved softly on her cheeks, blending with the free fall of her strawberry-blond curls. Sloane took pity on her.

"Ah . . ." he cleared his throat of its huskiness, "we'd better get going if we intend to get anywhere." His smirk was boyish and endearing, filling her with warm anticipation. A weekend alone with Sloane—nothing could sound more heavenly!

Justine relaxed back in her seat, reassured to know that her appearance pleased him . . . and disturbed him accordingly. The undercurrent of sexual excitement had always been strong between them, but never more so than at this moment. Once again the confines of the car conspired to heighten sensations that already ran high.

For better than an hour Sloane drove steadily, suffering as did she through the periodically stifling traffic. When at last they cleared the worst and left the parkway to negotiate the more private streets of Westport, the relief was tangible.

"Oh, it's lovely, Sloane," she exclaimed in response to the greenery which had gradually thickened with their approach. The land undulated gently in lushly alternating waves of maples, birches, beeches, oaks, and evergreens. "It's hard to believe that this country is less than fifty miles from Manhattan!"

"You've never been in Westport before?" The sidelong glance he gave her carried his surprise.

"No! I've been on Long Island many times, and I must have skirted this area during drives toward New England, but I've never had cause to stop. I can see what I've been missing!"

Enthusiasm lit her features as she took it all in—the richness of the landscape, the wealth of the homes as they bobbed up at intervals from one another, the cultured state of the streets themselves, and, at last, the Sound.

Sloane had turned in at a hidden drive and now followed the curving pavement through archway after archway of leafy green splendor until they reached the house. At first glance through the windshield it was beautiful. At second glance, when Justine stepped from the car and smiled in delight, it was magnificent.

"What do you think?" The deep voice came from immediately behind, drawing her head around in token recognition of his presence before she turned to study the house again.

"I think it's absolutely fantastic! I love it!" And she did! A distinctly contemporary structure, it was built of glass and fieldstone, with a shingled roof, large brown oak door and shutters, and a flagstone walk which beckoned irresistibly. Succumbing to its lead, she approached, breathlessly admiring the shrubbery with its patterned greens, whites, pinks, and purples, all flourishing under the skies of spring. "How did you ever manage to find this place?"

Sloane was close beside her, more intent on her reaction than on the sights she so admired. "It belonged to an author—he just wrote a best seller I'm sure you've heard about. . ." He laughed mischievously. "At any rate, he's off to Hollywood to do screenwriting for television. His loss—our gain."

Justine's eyes shone brilliant emerald when she looked up at him. *Our* gain, he had said—how natural it sounded! Had it been merely a slip of the tongue . . . or a figure of speech?

"Come on, let's go inside," he murmured softly, unlocking

the door, then taking her hand firmly in his. For Justine it was as though she were in a dream—being led by a silver-crowned vision of a man through the house of her fondest imaginings.

The foyer they entered was circular and open, giving access to a dining room and kitchen in one quadrant, a living room in another, the bedroom area in a third. Every room was spacious and modern, miraculously clean and freshly painted white. There were neither furnishings nor carpets; as they wandered slowly from room to room, their footsteps echoed in the emptiness.

"The best is yet to come," Sloane spoke warmly by her ear. "Those stairs"—he pointed to a stairway leading down—"why don't you go take a look while I start unloading the car. I'll meet you down there."

How anything could be better than what she had already seen she wasn't quite sure. Skeptically she followed his suggestion, however, slowly descending into the first floor of the house. Wordlessly she stopped, mouth agape, as she understood. Before her was a large, open room with a wall of solid glass which looked out upon the medley of early evening color that was Long Island Sound. Yellows and oranges skittered over the waves in long, rippling shards of light, blending with the gray of the water, the amber-hued stone and sand of the beach, and the darkening blue of the sky. It was a breathtakingly private moment for Justine, made even more precious by Sloane's silent arrival.

His arms slid around her gently as he joined her survey of the peaceful panorama. "Like it?" he murmured.

"Mmmmm." Words seemed inadequate. Her hand moved up to cover his, holding it against her waist.

"I'm glad."

For an eternity of silent appreciation they stood watching

and absorbing the glory of the seascape. Justine felt a sense of serenity flow through her, a sense of contentment she had never known. If preservation of the moment in all its heartfelt beauty had been in any way or form possible, she would have fought for it. But serenity was fleeting—as it would always be. Contentment was relative—as it too would always be.

Only the present was a fact. And the fact was the need she had to be totally one with Sloane. If she'd deprived herself in the past, she'd had good reason. Now that reason eluded her as her body strained toward fulfillment. Silent yearnings sparked then flamed, fed by the solid mass of lean and muscled masculinity which braced her back, her hips, her thighs.

Simultaneously Sloane felt the change. Turning her in his arms, he lowered his lips to kiss her softly. "I thought of you all the while I was away—picturing you here, wanting to hold you just like this. I need you, Justine. I—" The thought went unspoken as his attention was totally absorbed by her features, soft and open and overwhelmingly feminine in invitation.

She was a gentle spring flower, tall and slender, brandy-budded and ready to bloom. Sloane was her sun. It had been his riveting command which had sparked her growth, this sense of unfolding deep within, this sense of awakening. Now nothing less than his total possession would see it to fruition. He was the catalyst, the most moving force to have ever entered her life. For him alone was she willing to put aside past vows and bask in the moment's glory.

His kiss drew her inexorably closer to him. His sensual appeal was an intoxicant, pushing all other thought from mind. As he held her back for a long moment, his hands explored her curves, exhausting their outer limits before moving inward. He inspired total submission with his knowing touch, exacting helpless sighs from her as his fingers caressed the fullness of her breasts, made even firmer by his stimulation. Intuitively seductive, Justine strained against him, her arms velvet petals stretching up to cling to his neck. Whatever Sloane did to her she wanted; she wanted whatever he could give. Her life at that moment was Sloane; her being needed his for completion.

Her breasts glowed in creamy sheen when he slid the sweater over her head, then released the catch of her bra and discarded it quickly. The warmth of his hands sent quakes of desire through her, heightening a need which only he could fill.

But submission was not what he wanted. Taking her hand in his, he put it to his chest in silent command, urging her to touch him as he touched her. Instinct guided her fingers over and around the buttons of his shirt as, one by one, each was released. She gasped in wonder when the shirt fell to the floor, for it revealed a chest bronzed and broad, matted lightly with a T of gray-spiced curls that tapered to a narrow thread, then disappeared beneath the snap of his jeans.

"Go on," he urged softly, his urgency barely held in check. She touched him, timidly at first, then steadily thrilling to the glory of his body. Her fingertips traced a route from the leanness of his ribcage, made even leaner by his sharply sucked-in breath, to the dual swells of muscle which spanned his chest, then up and over the firmness of his well-padded shoulders. She moved in closer against him, reveling in the feel of her breasts, her nipples alive and taut, against the warm texture of him.

Again he spoke. "Wait here, sweetheart." She felt robbed of life when he moved away to crouch down on the floor and deftly spread the sleeping bags one on top of the other. "Our mattress." He smiled up at her, then held his hand out for her to take it.

In a moment of intruding reality, Justine realized the extent of what was about to take place. Her insides began to tremble, her limbs to quiver weakly. But she wanted Sloane. She needed him. His appeal to her feminine drive crushed all thought of future torment. There was fear and uncertainty—but only that she might not please him. Above all there was excitement and anticipation, the awareness that she was on the threshold of something new and wonderful. Her eyes held his, then dropped to the strong hand that reached for hers. Irrevocably she took it.

"Sloane," she whispered, sinking down onto her knees before him, "I've never . . . I haven't done this . . . I'm . . ." The words seemed all wrong and out of place, totally irrelevant amid the torrent of emotion which surrounded them. But she needed to tell him. Her green eyes were open and beseeching, her voice barely audible. "I've never been . . . with a man before. . . ."

Her pulse faltered, then raced ahead. It had been said. Would he laugh? Scowl? Think any less of her? He had no way of knowing why she had lived as chaste a life. He couldn't know of the hurt she'd suffered as a child and her resultant fear of an involvement to which sex was a potential stepping-stone. Now all that seemed secondary. But would he understand?

As she watched intently, his face took on a softer set than she had ever seen. His eyes, dark with desire, glowed with pleasure as well. He stared at her, seemingly unable to believe what she'd told him. When she shook her head slowly to reinforce the confession, he reached up and wound his fingers through her amber waves. Fierceness was tempered by wonder as he spoke low and husky. "Then I'm the first . . . to. . . ?"

She nodded silently, reasoning in part to herself. "Perhaps I shouldn't have said anything but . . . I thought you should know. . . ."

"My God, Justine! You're damned right I should know! It's not every day that a woman gives her virginity to a man." He paused, his thumbs caressing the corners of her quivering lips. "Are you sure, absolutely *sure*, that you want this?"

Her nod was slow and deliberate. "I want you, Sloane. Is it totally wanton of me to say that? I've never wanted anything as badly before. But I want you . . . I need you now." With growing confidence, she slid her hands across the flesh of his middle and around to his back, pulling herself closer to him. "Please, Sloane," she whispered softly, as a surge of intense desire seared her insides, "please make love to me."

He lowered his arms to imprison her in rapture, pressing against the small of her back such that she knew his desire was as great as hers. But he was slow and unhurried in his move to undress her, masterfully building her need, and his own, to a frenzied crescendo before finally laying her back and tugging off first hers, then his own jeans. His hand rubbed over the silken fabric of her panties, caressing her thighs, her stomach, all the searing hot contours between. Step by step, he led her, round and round the spiral of desire, ever higher, ever higher. When at last they lay, side by side, flesh against flesh, she felt aflame and about to burst. "Now . . . now, Sloane," she begged him shamelessly.

With a soft moan, he moved to blanket her with the warmth of his body, to absorb her pain, that pain that would be inevitable. At her helpless cry, he stilled, then held her tightly. "It's all right, sweetheart. That's all. It won't hurt anymore. I promise." Her short gasps slowly lengthened to a less agonized, more heady pace as a gentle exquisite warmth stole over her, bearing the first of the pleasure in its ever-widening wake. The flower had burst its bud and now opened, opened slowly and arched its way toward the sun.

With age-old rhythm Sloane moved above her, bidding her follow then join in perfect syncopation. He beckoned her higher, teaching her the joys of both her body and his as together they soared. Pleasure became glory, glory ecstasy, and then—a final explosion of utter fulfillment, a moment of supreme happiness surpassing all others. Their bodies were one, their minds were one; time stood still.

"I love you," she murmured breathless from the apex of her joy, "I love you, Sloane Harper." She had neither planned it nor expected it, yet the fact remained that she *was* in love. That had made the difference, she realized now. It was all new and had taken her by storm. She couldn't say it enough. "I love you." *This* was what it had all been about.

He lifted his head from its panting collapse on her shoulder and looked at her then, his skin damp and vibrant beneath her fingers. His heart beat in wild disturbance, but the grin that spread slowly across his lips left no room for doubt as to the pleasure she in her innocence had given him. "I *told* you we would be in agreement on everything, didn't I?" he crooned, his voice a deep rasp of emotion. "It's about time though. You certainly kept me waiting long enough!"

His smile was warm against her hair as he let his head fall forward once more. Beads of sweat mingled with the coppery wisps that framed her face.

"*Waiting long enough?*" she shrieked, light-headed. "My God, I've only known you for three weeks and a day—and most of that time you were on the far side of the continent! I'm even surprised you *did* make love to me"—she laughed softly, recalling another time when it might have been—"considering your thoughts about women who jump into bed with men they've known for *very short times!*"

"This was different." He laughed down at her, then rolled to the side and propped his head up on his palm. "I gave you plenty of time to think about it. That's one of the reasons I didn't call you while I was gone. I was afraid I might get carried away with sentimentality—"

"And what's wrong with sentimentality?"

"You're the prim and proper lady lawyer. *You* tell *me!*"

A frown crossed her brow as she feigned chagrin. "Hmmm, you're right. I haven't led a particularly sentimental life. Busy. Interesting. Rewarding. Challenging. But not terribly sentimental, is it?" Looking down, her eye caught the contour of his thigh, so firm and manly that she simply could not restrain the hand that reached out to mindlessly touch it. Caught up with fascination, she traced the tendoned length upward, then outlined the thin white markings where once a bathing suit had been.

"Oooo, lady," the voice above her inhaled sharply. "That's very dangerous . . ."

"But, I thought . . ." Her own eyes told her how misinformed she had been. "Sorry about that," she whispered, then caught his eye. She wasn't sorry at all. And her expression said it all.

With slow seduction, he met her unspoken challenge. And it was, to her astonishment, even more beautiful than before. If that first experience had been the blossoming, this second was the enrichment. With Sloane as a gentle and experienced guide, she learned how best to play his man's body and, in so doing, to fine-tune her own. When at last, as one, they reached that awesome pinnacle of ecstasy and tumbled over its edge in free fall, she felt that she had, indeed, become a woman.

Bodies intertwined, they slept, not to awaken until the last of the sun's flame had been banked for the night. Dusk was at hand, shrouding the world with its purple-hued mist. At its center, Justine glowed, wanned by love and passionately fulfilled.

"Hungry?" Sloane asked softly, turning to stroke the wayward curls from her temple.

"A little," she hummed softly.

His fingers were suddenly still, probing. "Hey, what's this?"

"That scar?" Her own slender forefinger joined his in confirmation.

"Yes, *that scar*. Where did *it* come from?"

"The school bus."

"School bus?"

"Uh-huh. Scott Anderson got angry because I called him a 'wimp,' so he threw his lunchbox at me."

"Why did you call him a 'wimp'?"

"Because he *was* one. At least, that was the meanest thing I could think to call him at the time. And he deserved it. He had hidden his bubble gum on the underside of one of my braids so that the teacher would not catch him chewing it. When we got on the bus, he decided he wanted it back. It was very painful!"

"I'll bet."

Justine raised her head as though hurt. "You don't sound terribly sympathetic, Sloane. Hmph! A lot of good you are!"

In the silence that followed, she curled into the waiting haven of Sloane's body and they lay together, quiet and at peace. "Tell me about yourself, Justine," he asked softly. "About your home, your parents, your experiences as a child . . ."

Keenly attuned to her mood, he felt her tension instantly. "Oh, you don't really want to hear about that," she scoffed evasively. "It's very humdrum."

"Fine. But tell me anyway. I know so little about that part of you." He hugged her even closer in a futile attempt to dispel her unease. "Where were you born?"

Any other subject would have pleased her more. "A hospital . . ."

"Where?"

His determination overrode her hesitancy for the time being. "A small town in Montana. You won't have heard of it. I grew up on the outskirts of Butte. Very ordinary."

"Your parents? Are they still alive?"

How strange it seemed to be sharing, after the fact, such personal information with a man with whom she had been so totally intimate already! In Sloane's arms, she forgot all else. Only her present with him mattered.

But *he* wanted to know more, and she couldn't deny him. "My mother died several years ago. My father is alive—he still lives in Montana."

"Why did *you* leave?"

Why did she leave? With painful memories of a childhood haunted by her parents' misery, the ugliness of their divorce and its lonely aftermath, she'd *had to* leave for her own survival. Besides, if, as a family law practitioner, she hoped to be able to help as many victims of similarly broken homes as possible, the big city was the place to be. "I felt that the opportunities for a lawyer would be better in New York," she answered simply. "I came east to college, then stayed on for law school. By that time I was pretty much addicted to the big city. What with the possibilities for employment beginning to open up for women, it seemed the logical decision." It had become easier to talk as the subject moved further from Montana—just as life had grown simpler with the distance.

"I'll bet you were a wild one, back in college," he teased her softly.

Her foot made contact with his solid shin as she kicked him in mock punishment. "You've just had proof to the contrary. How can you even suggest such a thing? I was a studier. That's all I did. Study. I won the hearts of all my teachers, made the dean's list every semester, and was accepted at the law school I wanted—Columbia. Very wild!"

Sloane laughed into the copper-colored curls which covered his shoulder. "I'm glad," he mused, then paused as he grew more serious. "What do you want out of life, Justine? In the long run, what do you want?"

On the surface it was an easy question. The answer had been her motivational force for years. Now, she answered with the strength of her conviction. "I want to be a *good* lawyer. I want to be respected as such. I want to continue to find the inner satisfaction I do now in my work. That's all . . . that's all." Her voice had lowered at the last and she frowned against the warm wall of his chest. That *was* all . . . yet, where did *this* fit in? Was there a place in her life for Sloane? Reluctant to brood on the future, she deftly turned the conversation around. "And what about you, Sloane? What do *you* want out of life?"

The length of his body grew even greater as he stretched lazily. She was not oblivious, however, to the thread of intensity which wound through him. "I want many of the same things, Justine. I want my business to flourish and its studies to benefit as many people as possible. I also want . . . a wife and children." Like a bomb, he dropped the last, leaving the silence to absorb its impact.

For a heart-shattering moment Justine knew an awesome fear. It was the same fear she had felt, though not recognized, the very first time she had met him. Periodically over the past three weeks it had returned in thin-wisped fragments to her consciousness. She hadn't understood it until now. Sloane represented a threat to her of the highest order. He wanted marriage . . . the one thing she wouldn't give him! She had seen her parents tear each other to bits. As the product of their unhappy union, she had herself been wrenched apart. Day after day she saw similar tragedies. Long ago she had decided that marriage had no place in her life. Love or no love, she would stick to her guns.

Sloane's voice was low and private. "Haven't you ever thought of children, Justine? Wouldn't you like to have them?"

She shrugged, willing indifference as she fought the turmoil within. "I've thought about it," she admitted—which, in fact, she had. But without a marriage there would be no children. She had accepted that and learned to live with it. "Work keeps me busy, though. And there's so much I want to see and do. You"— she poked his ribs as she steered toward safer ground—"travel a lot in your work. Some of us aren't that lucky. I'm just beginning to discover the beauty of traveling. I'd never been out of the country until I went to France last year. I spent a week in Paris . . . and loved every minute!"

Sloane was not fooled by her diversionary tactic; his prolonged silence, following her enthusiastic declaration, told her that. For some reason, however, he did not challenge her. Yet, his follow-up statement nearly took her back to square one. "You could travel with me whenever you liked. I'd love having you along. I've even got a big project coming up in—"

"But what do you do for *fun*?" Justine cut in, as much in desperation as in curiosity. Once again he hit too close to home, and she wanted nothing to spoil the time they shared.

His breath was warm, fanning her forehead. "I ravish fair maidens," he growled, disguising frustration in mischief.

"No, seriously, Sloane. You must have some hobby . . . do you play a sport. . . ?"

"Handball. I play as often as I can."

"Ah, that explains it, then. . . ."

"Explains what?"

"Your muscles." Rolling over onto him, she stretched to admire the subjects in question. "There had to be some work involved in building those . . . regular exercise, type-of-thing . . ."

Her eyes were as green as the new grass of spring beneath the sun's sparkle. Suddenly, she found herself on her back and looking up at the handsome face which hovered close above.

His hair was rich and full. On impulse, she threaded her fingers into its sterling sheen.

"Right now, I have a very different type of exercise in mind," he drawled, a return of huskiness in his voice. Just as Justine's senses came to life, however, he levered his taut-skinned form off her. "I believe I will take a jog. Into town. To pick up something to eat. I'm famished!"

His legs had already disappeared into his jeans, and he straightened to zip the fly. She could only stare at him in disbelief.

"Don't worry, sweetheart"—he read her mind exactly, swooping down to retrieve his shirt and croon playfully to her—"we'll have plenty of time later."

With a blush she sat up and wrapped the thick padding of the sleeping bag around her. "And what am I supposed to do while you jog into town?" Disappointed, she watched as he buttoned his shirt, robbing her of the heady sight of his chest.

"Why don't you jog with me?" he asked innocently.

"Because, in the first place, I don't jog. And, in the second place"—she squirmed slowly then grimaced—"I seem to be a little sore. I think I could use a hot bath."

The smile that lit his face was broad and hearty. "I suspected as much. And, you're in luck. I've brought towels. Let me get them while you run the water. Try the master bath upstairs—it's a sunken tub." His voice trailed off as he disappeared up the stairs toward the front door and the car. Justine was already half-submerged in a steaming tub when he returned carrying an armload of thick terry towels. "If you finish before I get back"—he winked from the bathroom door after dropping the towels and heading back out—"you can wander around and get some ideas for decorating. You'll have to earn your keep for the weekend somehow!"

Before she could find a suitable retort, he was gone.

Somehow. A warm flush seeped slowly upward as her thoughts turned to that *somehow.* How misleading life could be at times, she mused. Having always thought of herself as a feminist of sorts, she should have been soundly offended by his parting shot. *Earn her keep,* she laughed, particularly recalling the none-too-subtle leer which had accompanied that poignant *somehow.* Yet she felt no offense—none whatsoever. She had chosen freely to give herself to Sloane, and, in the process, had discovered that the giving was far from one-sided. Submission had never entered into their lovemaking. There had been giving and taking and sharing—all beautiful, all satisfying. Nothing would please her more than to spend the weekend in his arms!

As it happened, she did her share of amateur decorating as well. Much of Saturday was spent in this endeavor, as the two walked from room to room while Sloane noted her suggestions as to furniture, light fixtures, wall hangings and artwork, accessories, and floor treatment. "I would leave the windows as bare as possible"—she toyed with a concept that was totally out of the question in the city. "Privacy is not an issue here—you are surrounded by trees and ocean. Why not let it all in? Plants, perhaps—hang them there"—she pointed to the opposite ends of a wide window in the living room—"and there, but make sure that they complement the natural landscape rather than vie with it for attention."

"And the bedrooms. . . ?"

"There you'll need something for darkening effect alone. If, that is, you hope to sleep late once in a while. Otherwise, the bright sun pouring in at six may be a bit disturbing." She grinned, recalling how late they had slept this very morning, sun and all.

"We were *both* exhausted, sweetheart," he said, mirroring

her memory. "For my part"—a strong forearm fell across her shoulders—"I don't know whether it was work . . . or you."

Justine curled her arms around his waist, closing her eyes and resting her cheek against his chest. She inhaled deeply of his manly scent, then sighed her contentment. The moment was so beautiful, she mused. No past, no future—just now.

"Okay, to work!" Sloane ordered good-naturedly, setting her back from him. "I picked up cleaning supplies with lunch. What will you take—windows or bathrooms?"

"Windows." Given the choice of those particular two, Justine would do windows anyday!

"Coward," he taunted under his breath, as he handed her a cloth and a large spray bottle then selected his own and was off. At intervals they checked up on one another, with Justine starting on windows which were nearest the particular bathroom he scrubbed at a given time. After several hours they took a rest, walking the beach with carefree ease, enjoying the presence of each other and the mild ocean breeze.

Dinner was, by mutual choice, a joint endeavor. They had stocked the refrigerator and the cupboards with the basics—after Justine had wiped down the cabinets, inside and out, with Sloane calling directions from the last of the three bathrooms. "Nothing exotic," they had agreed, yet one thing had led to another, and, before they knew it, they sat down—in the bare middle of the shiny parquet of the dining room floor—to a dinner of London broil, baked stuffed potatoes, broccoli with hollandaise sauce, and peach melba. The irony of paper plates, plastic knives and forks, and the starkness of the empty room went by unnoticed. Hungry as they were, they ate. Romantic-minded as they were, they sipped fine wine from Dixie cups, grinning all the while. For Justine the dinner held as much elegance as any she had ever eaten.

Sloane lazed back on his elbow, stretched his legs their length and crossed them at the ankle as he watched her savor the last of her peach melba. "Do you have any idea," he finally asked, when every drop had been irrevocably consumed, "how many calories you've just consumed?"

She cocked her head defensively. "I said that I splurged once in a while. This happens to be that once!"

"And pizza last night?" he ribbed her, rolling his eyes skyward in memory. "I seem to recall that you matched me, bite for bite."

Tossing her head back at the unimportance of it, she grinned. "I daresay I've worked off every one of those calories." Bounding up, she loaded her hands with empty plates. "I'll have to see to that oven tomorrow. It badly needs a cleaning."

True to her word, the following afternoon found her head in the oven, her hands scrubbing. On a cold surface the spray was only marginally successful. Following the can's directions, she heated the oven, then set to it again. As she scrubbed diligently, her mind wandered. It came to her suddenly that she hadn't thought of law all weekend! In her adult life, this was a first! In case of emergency, Susan knew of her whereabouts. Yet, nothing had interrupted the bliss she had shared here with Sloane this weekend. The thought of its end, of returning to the city tonight, brought with it a knot of regret. Convinced of Sloane's love, she knew she would see him again and often. But, she mused, it had been so nice . . . so private . . . so quiet . . . here . . . alone with him.

"Justine!" Her own anticipatory frustration was embodied and intensified in Sloane's bellow. "Justine!" He stormed into the kitchen in time to see her reflexive flinch as her arm inadvertently came in solid contact with the heat of the oven shelf. "Where are the damned sleeping bags?" he shouted, then stopped. "Justine, are you all right?"

Doubled over, she slowly straightened and tried to stand,

fighting the stinging sensation on her arm. "I think I've burned myself. . . ." She grimaced, clutching the injured forearm. Sloane reacted intantly, pulling her swiftly toward the sink and thrusting her arm beneath the stream of cold water. "Ahhh . . . that feels a little better. . . ."

Engrossed as she was in an attempt to examine the damage, Justine was oblivious to Sloane's scowl. "How did you manage to do *this?*" It was a new and impatient Sloane, one she'd never seen before.

"I . . . I was startled when you . . . barged in here like that!"

"So it was *my* fault?" he challenged her darkly.

"Of course not!" she snapped back defensively. "I take full responsibility for my actions. It was my own dumb fault . . . and it's fine now, really it is." The arm was fine; oh, yes, it would probably turn into a minor blister before healing, but she felt no pain from *that* source. It was by Sloane that she felt injured.

He read the hurt in her soft and questioning green eyes, then turned the water off with a jerk and stepped back, combing his fingers carelessly through his hair. "Look, Justine. I'm sorry. I didn't mean to bark at you like that. It's just . . . trying to get things together before we go back . . ." He abbreviated his explanation, turning instead and heading for the door. "I feel really grubby, after scrubbing the patio. I'm going to take a shower."

Justine watched him disappear, her heart lodged somewhere between chest and mouth. Absently, she patted her arm dry with a paper towel, then stowed the cleaning supplies beneath the sink. Her brow bore a frown, her eyes a distinct look of worry. Could she let him stalk off like this? Why hadn't she said anything? After all, hadn't his gruffness been simply an expression of her own frustration? And, he *had* apologized.

Her hand slapped the counter determinedly as her sneaker-clad feet crossed the floor to follow him. The water was already running when she reached the bathroom, its air filled with billowing steam. Entering, then closing the door behind her, she leaned back against it, eyes mesmerized by the surrealism of the scene. Amid the mist she watched the shower door, its thickly textured glass a sensual conductor. Behind it Sloane welcomed the beat of the steady spray, turning slowly, throwing back his head, flexing his neck from side to side. His arms were bent at the elbows, his hands cocked surely on his hips. His skin took on a smoothly rippled texture through the shower door, investing her own fingertips with the yearning to touch as she had touched before. As he pivoted slowly, his every line was revealed to her, clear, then blurred, then clear again beyond the glass.

Driven by the new woman she had just discovered, Justine stepped carefully between his scattered clothes, peeled her own off, one by one, to join the pile, then approached and opened the shower door. The brunt of the spray was deflected from her by the sinewed breadth of his back as Sloane stared at her for several dark and heart-stopping moments. He seemed to be struggling, waging an inner war that she could only imagine. Then, before her wide-eyed watch a slow relaxation spread over his features until he resembled, at last, the man she adored. With a grin he took her in his arms, swinging her around and into the full spray of the shower, holding her there, despite her sputtering protest, until she was thoroughly soaked. Her hair was darker, truly copper when wet, and tumbled in tangled curls which he gently tucked behind her ears. When he kissed her, surrealism took on a different face, then burst quickly into blinding passion as desire washed over them both.

It was much later when he finally reached back to turn off the water. In the steam-shrouded silence, he held her body tightly against his, waiting as the last waves of ecstasy faded to loving memories. Her cheek was wet against his chest, her flesh against his as their heartbeats hammered through each other in one, nonending circle.

"Marry me, Justine," he murmured softly. "I want you for my wife."

Chapter 6

Stunned, she caught her breath . . . then waited . . . listened . . . wondered whether she had heard correctly . . . feared she had . . . yet prayed she'd only imagined it. Her heart told her she had not, even before the voice, deeper now and with conviction, came again.

"Will you marry me, Justine?"

His arms slipped in their hold to let her step back, though his palms snugly cupped her wet shoulders. She clung to his dripping features, adoring them with a sadness in her gaze, before averting her eyes to the blue and white tiling of the shower, still glistening with moisture. "It's a shame to have used it," she mumbled pathetically, "after you spent so long polishing—"

"Justine, did you hear what I said?" The fingers tightening on her flesh drew her attention back to Sloane's face. "That was a proposal. I just asked you to marry me. Will you?" His eyes were black as coal, yet soft, infinitely soft. For the first time in the whirlwind evolution of their relationship, she sensed a power that she, herself, held over this commanding and compelling man. It gave her no pleasure, only pain. To hurt him—to fail to give him anything, everything, he wanted—to deny him—was agony in itself.

"I . . . this is so . . . sudden . . ." she stammered, slipping easily from his wet grasp and stepping from the shower. She had wrapped her body in a bath sheet by the time his corded arm reached by her for the other that hung folded on the rack, the "his" to her "hers."

"There's nothing whatsoever sudden about it," he spoke softly, the frown which her fleeting glance detected his only outward symptom of disturbance. "After waiting thirty-nine years to find you, I would say that "sudden" is the last word I'd use to describe the situation."

"Precipitant, then. Impulsive . . ." She hung her head, groping defensively, blindly.

"When you gave yourself to me on Friday—when you surrendered that virginity you've held for twenty-nine years, was that on *impulse?*"

Her brows knit; she simply couldn't he. "No," she whispered.

"What was it then?"

Silence hung heavy in the sultry air. ". . . Desire . . ."

"Was that all?"

Again, she hesitated, sensing that she was slowly and inexorably being forced into a corner. *Hunted. Captured. Pinioned.* The image of the fox penetrated her consciousness with a force made awesome by the firm set of his jaw, the acute sharpness of his dark eyes, the full-headed lushness of his glistening silver hair. *The Silver Fox.* He would have to know it all . . . soon.

"I love you," she quietly voiced the depth of her feeling.

"Then marry me, Justine! You have no excuse not to!"

Whirling on her heel, she faced him. His towel was doubled

up and low-slung across his hips. Hands on the damp flesh just above, he stared at her, looming tall, much taller than he normally seemed to be. Intimidating at mildest, his physical presence threatened to wilt her. Quickly she fought to hold her head high.

"I can't. I won't, Sloane."

"Why not?"

"Because," she inhaled deeply, "I don't believe in marriage."

"Ah," he sighed and looked at the ceiling for a minute. "I remember you told me that once before. I let it pass then, but I will not now. What is so terrible about marriage?"

"It brings nothing but misery."

"That's not true—"

"It *is,* Sloane!" she interrupted forcefully. "I see it constantly in my work. Marriage seems to turn people hard and vindictive! It's marriage that—"

It was Sloane's turn to interrupt. "Not marriage, Justine. Love. Love . . . and the lack of it. If a marriage is built on love—as ours would be—the chances of success are high."

She shook her head sadly. "You don't understand.

"I understand that you're afraid. You're afraid to make a commitment to another person."

"That's ridiculous! I make commitments to people every day! When I take on a case, I make a commitment to that particular client."

The bridge of his nose drew taut with tension as he struggled for control. "There are many different kinds of commitment. I'm talking about the family kind . . . a husband . . . children—"

"No!" she shrieked unthinkingly, then quickly quieted. "I don't want to get married."

Sloane's patience seemed fast dwindling, as his rising voice implied. "Then what *do* you want? You say you love me, and you know that I love you. Where do we go from here, if not into marriage?"

Perspiration beaded thinly above her upper lip, born of nerves rather than the small room's slowly dissipating heat. This was the question she had refused to face as yet. Sloane was forcing the issue. "I don't know," she finally murmured in defeat.

"Well, that's just fine!" He raised his hands, then let them fall limp by his sides. "Would you suggest we just say 'good-bye' and go our separate ways—after this, this weekend?"

"No." The moist green pools of her eyes pleaded with him for some miraculous solution to the quandary.

"Then, what?" he prodded relentlessly, deep grooves carved by his mouth. "Should we just continue to have . . . an affair? Would you like to be my mistress . . . no further strings attached? Is that what would please you?"

"I—I don't know." Her voice was barely audible.

"Perhaps we should simply pass on the streets, in the corridors of your precious firm, and be good friends." His eyes suddenly took on a deeper tinge in passion's wake. "That would never work, Justine. I cannot see you"—he stepped closer—"without wanting to touch you"—he did—"to hold you"—he did—"to make love to you—"

She tore herself from his arms and fled to the bedroom, scooping up her clothes as she went. Sloane was close on her heels. "Running away from it won't do any good!" he roared. But, if he was nearing the end of his taut cord of control, Justine was no less so. Her body shook with tremors of emotion as she started to dress. His bellow shook her even more. "I *love* you, you fool! Doesn't that mean anything to you?"

"It's not enough!" she yelled, an equal partner now in the shouting match. "The odds are still against us!"

Suddenly, he grew more calm. "But aren't they worth risking? Isn't the end result worth taking the chance?" It was his quiet pleading that finally broke her.

"I can't," she whispered, tears filling her eyes and tightening her throat. As her cheeks grew wet, she turned away from him, hugging her stomach protectively. In the silence that followed, she wondered if he had given up. She flinched when he stepped around in front of her, clad only in his jeans, his feet and upper torso bare.

"There's something else, isn't there? Something you haven't told me." He paused, calculating her air of dejection, sensing confirmation of his suspicion in her lack of denial. "What is it, Justine? It has to do with . . . your family, doesn't it?"

When she tried to turn from him, he held her, his strong hands gentle but firm on her arms. Head bent, she shook it, refusing to confront that old pain. But Sloane was persistent. "I have a right to know, Justine. I love you. I want you to be *my* family, to help me *make my* family. You are a seeker of the truth, aren't you? Then respect my need for it, too. If you're asking me to settle for something less than what my heart wants, you owe me this much."

She could fight him no longer. Inching away from him, she moved the short distance to the wall, propped her back against it, and slid down until she sat at its base, knees bent up, arms clamped tightly around them. "My parents fought from the earliest time I could remember," she began, releasing the hold on her mind, letting it make the agonizing journey back over the years. "My father was a businessman, trying to get started. Money was a constant issue between them. My mother had patience for neither my father nor me." She looked up sadly at Sloane. "I took after him—the hair coloring and all." That very coloring, vivid now in hair dried freely and with benefit of neither comb nor brush, gave her a frail, waiflike air. She felt, indeed, small and vulnerable.

"They separated when I was eight, divorced when I was nine. In the meantime, I was shuttled back and forth between neighbors and relatives, never quite knowing where I would be spending the next week, month, or year. I . . ." She faltered, recalling those years of insecurity so sharply. "I withdrew into myself . . . buried myself in fantasy as much as was possible. It was a difficult situation, you see. My father wanted me, but it was my mother who had the money—her family's money—to raise me in the style she felt I should be raised. My mother didn't want *me*; she simply didn't want my father to have me! So I was bounced around for a while."

Breathing deeply, she forced herself to retain some measure of composure. The tears had dried, yet she felt on edge. Sloane had not said a word; his tall form was ramrod straight, his hands thrust in the pockets of his jeans, their balled fists clearly marked. The muscle of his jaw moved once, then again. "Go on." *His traditional command,* she mused somberly, recalling other times when he had used it. As in those cases, she acquiesced.

"It finally went to court. I was the star witness. What was it like living at home? they asked me. Were my parents good to me? Could I talk with my mother? With my father? Whom did I feel most comfortable with? Had anyone ever struck me? Did *he* read me good-night stories? Did *she* sit down at night and comb my hair?" Closing her eyes, she pictured that nightmare, reliving it and its pain once more. "They kept repeating that everyone should remember that I was only nine years old. What did I know about things? they implied. Well"—she turned her gaze, strong and venom-filled, at Sloane—"I knew plenty! I knew the guilt of having to testify in favor of, then against, a parent. I knew the confusion of being pulled from both ends. I knew the fear of punishment, of reprisal. I was terrified!"

Her eyes, in all their emerald sharpness, reflected that terror, bringing Sloane down to kneel before her and stroke her cheek. "I'm sorry, Justine. I didn't know—"

"There's more!" she exclaimed, suddenly angry at having been forced into the declaration. "You wanted to hear? Well, there's more. You see, not only did I hear my parents' arguments, but I heard the gossip of the neighbors. My mother was a selfish witch, they said, who only wanted to cover her own mistake— the mistake being marrying my father in the first place. I was the major pawn; she also wanted to recover the money her family had invested in his business. Make him suffer. After all, they said, *he* was out having a good time. The 'Red Rover,' they called him on occasion. Fast and wild with the women, they said. A rogue . . . a dandy . . . you name it. I heard it all, but somewhere, deep inside, I knew that he loved me."

Suddenly, she was crying again. Soft sobs escaped her lips as she buried her face against her knees. Sloane's hand massaged her neck, his fingers working on the tautness there.

"I'm sure he did, Justine," he crooned gently. "What finally happened? I want to hear it all."

"My mother was given custody, at which point she handed me over to whoever was willing to keep an eye on me for a year or two. Aunts, cousins—I finally spent most of my teenage years with a great-aunt. Then, I came east to college and . . . you know the rest."

Having bared herself of the sordid story, she felt relieved. Her body yielded as Sloane drew her closer against him, and she succumbed to his comforting warmth. "Did you see your father much?"

"Never. *She* saw to that! Even though she didn't care to spend much time with me herself, she was determined that he should never see me. When I was a child, I was too young to know any better. I didn't fight the edict. As I grew older, I always wondered about him but ... I was ... I still am ... frightened. There's always that chance that he didn't really want me either—that I reminded *him* of *her*—that *he* wanted me simply because she said *she* did!" She shook her head against his chest. "It's all very ugly."

"So you've made it your life's work to help people—children— who are put in similar positions?"

His perceptivity stunned her. She hadn't quite expected him to make the connection as quickly as he had. "Yes. I have."

"And in the process," his voice hardened noticeably, "you see only the negative in marriage. You've surrounded yourself with failures. You refuse to look at the others—the successes."

"No, it's not that at all—"

"Isn't it?" he growled dangerously, holding her back and spearing her with his daggered look. "It's self-reinforcing— your work. What we have here is a self-fulfilling prophesy once removed. You see failure after failure and are now totally convinced that that's all there is." Justine could only stare in shock at Sloane's rising anger. They had come full circle; was it possible he could not understand what she was trying to say? His next words were in apparent proof of this. "You *are* afraid, Justine. I've heard your story and, as painful as it must have been, the living of it is only an excuse. The fact that you remained a virgin for twenty-nine years then gave that virginity to me should tell you something. . . ." He stood tall now, drawn high in conviction. "But you're afraid to take the greater chance. Evidently you don't love me enough!" With a final glower of dismissal, he stalked from the room, his bare feet echoing on the flooring in ever-fading pads.

At that instant something within Justine shriveled and died. It was as though she were a balloon, inflated, inflated, inflated, with each breath a bit of the fullness Sloane brought to her life—then suddenly, the air sputtered madly out, leaving her hopelessly empty, totally drained. Happiness burst before Sloane's dark accusation. She didn't love him enough? Was that why the pain inside grew ever larger, to replace that awesome void?

A month passed with no word from Sloane. It was, for Justine, a month as tedious as any she had ever spent. For her life was strangely dichotomized, with gross distinctions between the lawyer Justine and the woman Justine, and an ongoing war, albeit cold, between the two. There was the Justine O'Neill who entered, with determination, the domain of Ivy, Gates and Logan every morning, who conducted her meetings with clients and attorneys in her usually efficient and humanistic way, who operated in the courtroom with the same aplomb for which she had become known. Then, however, there was the Justine O'Neill who returned home alone at night tired, discouraged, lonely, restless, and seemingly unable to rally her private wits about her.

Over and over she relived the weekend in Westport, its love, its passion, and, finally, its grief. Sloane would simply not compromise, it appeared, if the month's silence was any indication of his intent. Either she would marry him . . . or their relationship was at an end. Such seemed the ultimatum he had wordlessly given her. Though her heart ached inconsolably, she was unable to give in. There had been too much anguish in her past; she saw too much of it in her present. She wanted freedom from that particular torment. Unfortunately, in choosing that freedom she had unknowingly opted for a different brand of torment, one that came from deep within and robbed her of the ability to smile.

"You're looking very sober lately, Justine." John stood at the door of her office late one afternoon, when most of the firm had left for the night. "Overworked?"

"No more so than usual." Her hand continued to move across the page, her pen making notes for a speech she was scheduled to deliver the following morning.

"Then you aren't getting enough sleep. You look tired." Having invited himself in, he now sat leisurely in the chair before her desk.

"Anything else you'd like to tell me?" She glanced up quickly, her sarcasm coated with fatigue. "I love it when you say such nice things."

"I wasn't trying to be 'nice.' You do look tired. Man troubles?"

"No."

"Too fast." He caught her. "That came out a bit too fast. Is it Sloane?"

"I haven't seen Sloane in weeks." Her pen bore the brunt of the teeth she sank into its tip.

John's blue eyes harrowed in hint of amusement. "So that's the trouble."

"John," she sighed wearily, putting the pen down with a snap, "I'm really not in the mood for discussing this. It's been a very bad day. Please—" Her throat felt suddenly strained, and, for a horrifying moment, she thought she would cry. Tears had been all too common in her private hours; up until now she had mercifully managed to keep them private. With every bit of her willpower, she swallowed convulsively, ordering herself to maintain composure. It worked, though her struggle did not go unnoticed by her colleague.

"He may just be playing it cool, you know. Men do that sometimes. And the fox—the fox is an expert at avoiding the trap."

Justine's sharp laugh was a surprise to even her. Though it was devoid of humor, it was the first such sound she'd made in days. *Avoiding the trap,* she mused—he *was* the trap!

Misinterpreting her response as a sign of encouragement, a hint of her opening up on the matter, John continued. "The fox has unique methods of breaking the line of scent, of misleading and confounding all those after him." She lifted a shaped eyebrow in curiosity, unconsciously egging him on. "Sure. He stops in his tracks, turns around, retraces them for a while, turns front again and moves ahead just a fraction of that distance—then suddenly bounds sideways, off the track, preferably into a stream or onto the top of a fence, and runs off."

"Fascinating," she grumbled facetiously, wondering just how she had managed to find this wildlife expert—or he, her.

"He even manages to hop onto the back of a sheep once in a while, to hook a free ride, track free, then jump off when the coast is clear. Very clever, if I don't say so myself." He smiled, so caught up with his discourse that her frown was ignored.

That frown, however, was becoming a semipermanent fixture on Justine's face. It was particularly noticeable at home, where she had usually been so relaxed. Susan was concerned.

"Are you feeling okay?" she asked one Sunday morning in good nursely fashion when she tired of watching Justine roam idly around the apartment in uncharacteristic avoidance of the mouth-watering Sunday edition of *The New York Times.* Usually there was good-humored rivalry about who read which section first. On this particular morning Susan had the paper all to herself. "You're not getting sick, are you?"

"No, Sue. I'm fine. Really." Her eyes were glued to the street below, seeing nothing, yet mesmerized by the occasional movement of life there.

"Things been tough at the office?"

"Mmmmm."

And, after a pause—"No word from Sloane?"

Justine shuddered lightly before recovering herself. "No."

"Look, Justine. Maybe you should get away for a while. It's nearly the end of June. You were planning on taking a few weeks in August anyway. Why not move them up?"

Vacation? What good would vacation do, if the demon was within? Was there any escape? "No, Susan. It's probably better if I work. I'm just tired now. The Fourth is coming up—I'll have a short vacation then."

How easy it was, she mused, to give pat answers to questions whose crux was much deeper! How simple it was to put off the expressions of concern—to keep friends and colleagues on the outside, at a safe distance from her turmoil. Only Sloane had penetrated her thick-skinned veneer; only he had stolen into her heart. In hindsight, she marveled at his cunning, yes, his *cunning* in captivating her. Their explosive physical attraction had been mutual; that had helped his cause. But he had stalked her with such brilliance, such laid-back persistence, that she couldn't have recognized her growing love if it had been waved before her clear, emerald eyes.

Her love for Sloane was a fact, but a sadly deficient one. As Sloane himself had said that last day in Westport, she must not love him enough if she still refused to marry him. Perhaps he was right. But, she asked herself poignantly, what about *his* love for her? What was *its* nature, that he could sever all contact with her of his own free will? Was this, as John had consolingly suggested, a tactic? Was he merely exercising the sharp-honed intelligence for which the fox was known? His parting words to her that fateful Sunday afternoon when he pulled to a brusque stop outside her apartment building had been a curt "I'll contact you," but they had been his *only* words of that seemingly endless drive from Westport to Manhattan and had been delivered with an undertone of pure business. Had he something in mind?

Indeed, he did. The Silver Fox was not to be underestimated. "Justine"—Daniel Logan's summons vibrated firmly over the intra-office line—"I've got Sloane Harper in here. Could you join us for a moment?"

Any other member of the firm she might have been able to put off; Dan Logan she could not. Surely Sloane Harper would have known that! And surely, she simmered in frustration, he would have to know how potentially uncomfortable a public confrontation would be for her—recalling in vivid detail how intimate their last confrontation had been.

Standing weakly, she tugged at her skirt and smoothed down the soft folds of her blouse. The early summer's heat seemed to have suddenly penetrated even the air-conditioned confines of the office, choking her at the throat, the wrist, the waist—at every spot where her clothes touched her body. But the inevitable had to be faced. Mustering the shreds of a nearly nonexistent self-possession, she walked the route to the senior partner's office—wondering all the while what nature of weapon the firing squad would use.

"Excuse me?" she heard herself say moments later as she sat straight-backed in Dan's office. Sloane was far to her right, nearly behind her, standing, watching, alert. Other than a perfunctory word of greeting upon her arrival, he had not spoken.

"That's right, Justine," Dan repeated patiently. "We would like you to accompany Sloane to Alaska for the preliminary work on his project."

Eyes paler green in disbelief, Justine looked from Dan to Sloane, then over to Charlie Stockburne. "I don't—I don't understand. What use would I be to Sloane in Alaska? I don't know anything about the corporate end of the law. Certainly it would be more appropriate if one of the others went." Pulse racing, she focused her attention on Dan, excluding Sloane's stern expression as much as possible. Having known his warmth, his tenderness, his love, this near formality was a torture.

"Perhaps you've misunderstood me, Justine." Dan eyed her sharply, his gaze, in its reproof, saying far more than his words. "Sloane proposes to use you as a consultant on the project he is planning. You won't be actually acting as his lawyer on *behalf* of the corporation, but rather—"

"—as an employee of the corporation—" she interrupted on a soft note of dismay at the gist of the suggestion.

"'Consultant' is a more dignified word, Justine." Sloane finally entered the ring, throwing down the gauntlet with his unique air of majesty. Slowly and with characteristic dignity, he approached her. "I feel that, with your background in family law, you might be of help. Are you at all familiar with the situation of economics in Alaska?"

Helpless as the walls began to close in around her, Justine shook her head. So this would be her punishment for refusing to marry him—a sentence of subservience as his underling? To be near, yet just beyond reach—was this what he had in mind? Fighting to quell the churning within, she willed her attention to what Sloane was saying.

"Since the advent of the oil pipeline, Alaska has, to state it simply, come into a lot of money. The question is how to most suitably spend it—or invest it—such that the people of the state receive the greatest long-range benefit."

"And your job?" she probed, interested despite herself.

"CORE International has been retained by the state of Alaska to determine the areas of greatest need. It will be our job to canvas the state, identify what we believe to be the most serious deficiencies in social, educational, custodial services, then make proposals for a course of action to remedy them."

"Very impressive," she murmured, "and exciting"—then quickly remembered herself—"but I still feel that any one of the men would be more suited to accompany you than I would be. And, frankly, I don't see how I could fit this into my schedule."

Dan eyed her reproachfully. "On the contrary. Many of the courts are closed during the summer months. And you'll have enough time to rearrange your speaking engagements, alert clients, redirect appointments. There are plenty of people here who can cover for you. And, I believe"—he challenged her to deny his claim—"you were planning to take several weeks off in August anyway. Am I wrong?"

"August?" Was that when this fiasco was scheduled to take place? "Ah, no, you aren't wrong. I *was* planning to take off time then." She punctuated her emphasis on the past tense with a pointed glance Sloane's way. "When is this Alaska trip scheduled?"

It was the tall, silver-haired keeper of her heart who answered in a clear, deep tone. "We are planning to spend the entire month up there. Any problem?" A manly brow arched into lines on his forehead, lines she had never noticed before. In fact, as she stared closely now, there were other lines she hadn't noticed. He looked wan, tired—as she felt.

"A month?" Her heart fell another notch. "Four weeks? I don't know"—her strawberry-blond curls jiggled with her tentative headshake—"that's a stretch. To be gone from the office for that length of time—"

"Justine"—her attention flew to Dan—"this matter is not exactly up for your debate." He seemed to be more ruffled, less patient. Was he, too, uncomfortable with the proposal? If so, he was equally as uncomfortable with her hesitancy. "As a member of this firm, it is in your best interest to make what-ever arrangements are necessary to prepare for the trip. Sloane will fill you in on the details. There will be several briefings beforehand. I believe he can tell you what clothing would be appropriate for summer in Alaska—I certainly can't!" He chuckled wryly.

Justine found no humor in his quip. "Then I have no choice? This is an order? It's either go . . . or . . ." she gestured toward the door with her thumb, her eyes flaring in anger and disbelief, ". . . leave?"

The only comfort came from Charlie, who had moved up from behind and propped himself on the arm of her chair. She watched as Sloane moved away, then looked up at the lawyer. "It's not as ominous as you make it sound, Justine," he began soothingly. "You are a partner in the firm. Obviously, you have a say. What Dan is saying, I think"—he glanced quickly at the other for support,—"is that, of the partners, we feel you to be the best qualified to accompany Sloane." Her peripheral vision caught the client in question Standing, back to her, facing the window. Charlie continued. "If making the trip is going to cause a major upheaval to your schedule, we can reconsider. It is *your* choice."

A bit of the fox in everyone, she had reflected once. Here was a perfect example; Charles Stockburne had slyly presented his case. Indeed, it was her decision to make—whether she should make the trip to Alaska with Sloane. But what really was her choice? Dan Logan was still the undisputed power in the firm, and *he* obviously had determined that she go. If she balked? Would her own place in the firm then be endangered? Was it a chance she should take?

And if she went—her eyes flew to the broad back across the room—what might that mean? It would mean, she realized with bristling annoyance, that Sloane had succeeded in manipulating her once more. What would he expect of her en route? What would *she*, perhaps, want? In the worst of her worries, she might well betray herself, knowing how deeply his presence affected her. Even now, as she stared, he turned slowly, a sterling icon of virility, and sent a shuddering message to and through her.

"Perhaps," she began unsurely, clearing her throat, and tearing her gaze from his to face the others, "perhaps I might speak with Sloane more in detail. I have quite a few questions, many of which might bore you two."

The senior partner, sensing her indecision, knowing that Sloane was, in the end, his own best advocate, acceded to her request. "Of course, Justine. That sounds like a fine idea. Would you like to use this office?"

"No"—she jumped quickly to her feet, then regretted it instantly as her knees silently rebelled—"my own office would be better, I think. That way I can take notes . . . check my calendar . . . that kind of thing . . ." On her home turf she would feel safer. The important thing, she mused, was to get away from these two other men and isolate Sloane. Much as she questioned the wisdom of being alone with him, there were too many personal issues involved to remain here. Mustering her strength, she nodded to Dan and Charlie, then led the way back down that long, long hall.

Sloane Harper was beside her every step of the way, his lithe, lean frame slowing his strides to match her shorter ones. His personal aura surrounded her, crisping her senses, giving her second thoughts as to what in the world she was doing, daring her heart to stand up against him. Relieving unsteady legs of their meager burden, she settled into the chair behind her desk, then watched as Sloane shut the door and lounged back against it, hands thrust casually in his pockets, a distinctly smug grin on his face. *He was handsome,* every whimsical sense screamed within her, at war with those instincts of reason which stiffened her back.

"What are *you* grinning at?" she snapped testily. "I don't think I dropped anything this time—and I didn't trip over myself. What else could possibly be funny?" *Other than the fact,* she acknowledged with silent reluctance, *that you have planned this farce as a demonstration of your power! Were you that injured at my refusal to marry you,* she wondered, *that your need for revenge has come to . . . this?* "What is it you want, Sloane?"

His smile was undaunted by her attempted freeze. "How have you been, Justine?"

"Fine." She held his gaze unwaveringly, gaining strength in her anger, power in her hurt.

"You look tired."

"I am. And, so do you—look tired—by the way."

"I am—too."

Was it to be a battle of words as well? With a sigh, she took the offensive. "Then, let's make this brief. What do you *really* want? This trip and all—what does it mean?"

"I want your legal expertise, Justine. Nothing more." The cooling of his own tone did not go unnoticed, nor did the straightening of his body.

"Come on," she goaded him. "It can't be just that. Any other lawyer would have served as well. Why me?"

Despite his alertness, he was the picture of innocence. His face was devoid now of smugness, his eyes of sensuality. For a minute she wanted to believe him. "I think you may be the best in this field," he announced simply. "You know your law and you're creative in applying it. In my work I go for the cream of the crop. You already know that. What more would you have me say?"

Her eyes narrowed in lingering skepticism. "I want to know what's going on in that crafty mind of yours—below the surface. You haven't called me in a month. Now, you pop right in and deftly maneuver my exile for a month. This is *my* life, Sloane. You can't just—" Suddenly, in a flash of realization, she understood. A slow simmer lowered her voice dangerously. "That's it, isn't it? You want me away. Away from this—my work— the dealing with divorce every day." Recollection of their last, prolonged discussion was instantly fresh; "You consider this to be an unhealthy atmosphere for me. Is that it?" Tapered fingernails dug into the soft flesh of her palm; with deliberation, she unclenched her fist and laid her hands flat on her desk.

Sloane, on the other hand, was maddeningly calm. Several fluid steps brought him from the door. "And what if it is true? Would it make much difference? After all, we're only talking about a month."

"A month of my very personal time!" she cried out in frustration, realizing that he had, with characteristic cunning, avoided a direct confession.

He grew more sober. "I'm sure you'll be able to take your vacation later—"

"That's not the point!" She paused, catching her breath, suddenly overcome by fatigue and courting the germs of a headache. With merciful diversion, the telephone console flickered. "Yes, Angie...? No, I'd rather not take any—who...? Yes, put him on."

Swiveling her chair such that its back was to Sloane, she spoke softly into the receiver. "Hi, Tony...! Not bad... Yes, I heard.... I'm glad.... Tonight...? No, uh, yes, I'd like that.... I am, but I'll be fine.... Good.... See you later." The conversation had been quiet, its end in a near whisper. For long moments after Tony hung up, Justine held the phone against her. There was that special bond between them, and she badly needed someone to talk to. Perhaps he might be able to help her sort things out; if all else failed, his would be a welcome shoulder to cry on.

Swiveling back front, Justine caught the dark look on Sloane's face moments before his voice grated across the short distance. "Who is Tony?"

"Tony is a very special friend." Fresh upon what she felt to be Sloane's betrayal of her, she had no intention of spelling out the true nature of the relationship. Half in spite, she added a pointed "I'm having dinner with him tonight."

"So I gathered." He hardened then, growing all business. "Look, there will be a meeting the week after next at my head-quarters. You'll be able to meet the others then—" He caught her surprise. "—Yes, there will be others along on the trip." A wry smile thinned his lips. "Two others on this initial team. I'll have more details at that meeting. Can you make it?"

Pouting seemed inappropriate. "I suppose so," she stated calmly.

"Good." He turned to leave. "I'll have some preliminary materials sent over for you to examine. And . . . Justine . . ."—it was the first true note of gentleness she had heard and she subconsciously perked up—". . . try to get some rest."

"You, too," she called flippantly, then, when he was no longer in sight, whispered more softly, "You, too."

Tony was, indeed, a good listener, though he was far from sympathetic on all scores. Justine had already told him about Sloane, so the fact that she had fallen in love was no surprise to him. For the first time, however, she related Sloane's proposal of marriage and her subsequent refusal. *That* drew out the brotherly instinct.

"Are you sure you've made the right decision, Justine?" he

asked. "I mean"—his eyes fell for a moment of hesitancy—"we haven't ever really gone into all that, but I know how badly you were hurt by Dad and your mother. I'm not quite sure, though, that you should let that one instance sour your feelings forever."

To the best of her ability she argued her case, talking of her work and its lessons. And, though Tony did not broach the matter of the ugly experience of her childhood again, neither was he convinced of the justification for her beliefs. On the issue of Alaska he pointed out the positive, exuding excitement at the prospect of such a trip, such an experience. His mood was contagious; by the time he had kissed her good-bye at her apartment door, pleading an excess of coffee and an early appointment the next morning, she felt buoyed. Once again, however, the bubble burst as soon as she was left to her own psychological devices. Where the heart was concerned, she was fast discovering, reason was irrevocably altered.

As she approached the law so she approached her dilemma. The facts, as she saw them, were easily laid out. There was the fact that she loved Sloane and he loved her; their weekend in Westport had proven that decisively. There was the fact of his marriage proposal and her refusal; again, these were absolute. There was the fact of the CORE International project in Alaska and her own abduction into its realm. But there the facts ended.

From there things grew muddled. Fine lines blended together, confusing issues, complicating others. What were the offshoots of these facts? Would their love lead them to a viable compromise? Could Sloane discover that he might temporarily abandon the thought of marriage if being with her meant enough to him? Would this trip to Alaska be the deciding force *for* or *against* their future? What was that future to hold?

Above it all Justine only knew that Sloane's appearance in her life had brought with it the kind of upheaval she had never, in her well-paced designs, envisioned. To her chagrin she was ill prepared for it. Her emotional keel wavered left to right, high to low. There seemed no stable force to cling to. *Until that day,* a mere one before the meeting at Sloane's office, when she found that force around which to rally.

On that day, in early July, she discovered she was pregnant.

Chapter 7

"You're *what?*" It was seven thirty in the morning. Susan Bovary had just returned from working her usual night shift. She was exhausted, to say the least, and now wondered if she'd heard correctly.

"I'm pregnant." Justine calmly repeated her announcement, eyes sparkling, lips twitching up at the corners despite her own sleepless night. Still in her robe, she intended to spend the morning in bed. Her meeting with Sloane was not until one in the afternoon. She owed herself this small luxury—and she badly needed the rest.

Susan was suddenly wide awake. "You're pregnant? You're going to have Sloane's baby?"

"*My* baby, Sue." She smiled gently. "And yes, I *am* going to have it."

Her roommate's eyes clouded momentarily. "Are you . . . pleased?"

Justine's continuing smile and the light flush on her cheeks heralded her answer. The night had been one of soul-searching. She'd been shocked at first, then terrified at the thought of being pregnant. And alone. From the first that was a given. But as the hours wore on, her mind had warmed to the thought of the microscopic seed growing in her body. Yes, she had alternatives and she considered each in turn. She could agree to marry Sloane . . . but she wouldn't. She could easily arrange for an abortion . . . but she couldn't. Hence her decision was made. Her future would hold love after all. She'd love her child with every ounce of her being.

She hadn't anticipated getting pregnant, hadn't planned on having a child. But it was marriage that frightened her even more than motherhood. Now she carried Sloane's child, a child conceived in love. That knowledge gave a glow to her smile.

"After nearly eighteen hours of nonstop deliberation . . . yes, I'm pleased. In fact I'm feeling very . . . lightheaded."

Her joy was evident, much as it surprised Susan. "Oh, Justine, I'm thrilled for you then! I had no idea you wanted a baby."

"Neither did I," her friend retorted with humor. "And I was pretty shocked at first. Since I saw the doctor yesterday, I've had to totally rethink my plans. I do intend to have the baby and I plan to raise it myself."

"Yourself? You mean"—Susan started in disbelief—"that you still won't marry Sloane?"

"No." Soft but firm.

"But . . . what if he wants the baby?"

"He won't necessarily know about it—"

"You're not going to even *tell* him? Justine, it's his child, too! He has a right to know!"

"That's where I don't agree with you," Justine argued, voicing her thoughts of the night gone by. "When Sloane realized that I wouldn't marry him, he more or less deserted me. I didn't hear from or about him for a full month. Then, I finally saw him in the office, and there was some harebrained scheme for me to act as the lawyer-specialist for his project. Well, I'll go with him to Alaska, and I'll give him the best legal advice I can. But that's all. After the month we will have nothing to do with one another."

"But he'll see—"

Justine shook her pale-copper-covered head. "I've got it all figured out, Sue." Her eyes reflected her excitement, gleaming a rich green beneath a thick red fringe. "I'm barely six weeks pregnant now. The trip is planned for August. I'll only be in my third month then, into my fourth at the end of the trip." Her voice quickened with anticipation. "The doctor told me that, with a first pregnancy, I probably wouldn't show until the end of the fourth or the fifth. If that's the case, Sloane will never know. And, I have this funny feeling that I won't be wearing the chicest of outfits there in the wilds of Alaska. All I have to do is to pick loose things, sweaters and jackets that hang fairly full and low. Very simple."

Susan eyed her skeptically. "*If* he never sees you nude—"

"He won't!" It was a seething vow, reflective of the hurt Justine continued to feel inside along with her love for Sloane. Now, she had the baby to consider; instantly the thought soothed her.

Susan was quiet for a moment, before moving on. "And what about work—when you do show?"

Again, Justine had considered this. "I think that, given proper camouflage, I can work until my sixth month. Then, I will simply take a leave of absence. If the firm can so easily spare me for this month"—her dismay at the last fact surfaced unbidden—"they can just manage without me for a while longer. Then, I will find a nurse to take care of the baby during the day—when I decide to go back to work."

"But the law . . . it's always meant so much to you, Justine. Will you be able to handle it?"

There was a flicker of doubt, of unsureness, in Justine's gaze.

"I hope so, Sue. I'm certainly going to try," she answered Susan as honestly as she could. "I do know that I want this baby . . . almost as much as I've always wanted that career. If determination is all that counts, I'll manage fine."

The smile that her roommate bestowed upon her was filled with hope, tinged with skepticism. Justine accepted it, knowing it was only the first of many such friendly expressions of doubt she might expect. But she had to be prepared. Her life had undergone a total emotional reversal in the past hours; it was up to her to set her course and follow it faithfully.

When she arrived in Sloane's office, a well-planned and decorated room in an ultramodern suite of offices, she was fully composed. Only the charcoal smudges beneath her eyes told of her need for rest. But that would come, she told herself. It was simply a matter of settling into a schedule once more. As for her eyes, her cheeks, her lips—they were full of life, bright and glowing, radiating the warmth she felt at the thought of the seed—Sloane's seed—that grew inside her.

"You're looking better," he commented, staring hard at her when she arrived. For a moment of heart-stopping hesitation, she wondered if he could tell—or might guess—her secret. But the meeting went on without delay, setting her mind at ease. Having read the preliminary material Sloane had sent to her office, she could readily follow the directives he gave now. Taking notes on her long legal pad, she engrossed herself in the work, denying the very presence of the man whose lean frame was never far from her, whose eyes were uncomfortably keen and attentive, whose thick head of silver hair haloed about him deceptively.

Her seeming immunity to his manly appeal gave her courage—and the growing belief that she might just pull it off! The next few weeks passed, similarly without a hitch, further buoying her. In the presence of others, Sloane, it appeared, presented no threat to her sensibilities. So she told herself—over and over and over again at every weak moment of self-doubt.

The chore of shopping for clothing for the trip was simplified by the list which Sloane provided. In great detail it outlined the necessities—down parka and heavy denims, woolen socks, flannel shirts, mittens, long underwear, knit hat—that the chill of the Arctic nights, even these at the end of the northern summer, might require. Justine carefully selected items that left room for growth, though her stomach remained as flat, her waist as narrow, as they had always been.

Having settled the basics in her mind regarding her pregnancy, she was determined not to worry. If Ivy, Gates and Logan balked at her plans, there would be other firms, other opportunities. Thanks to the professional reputation she had already established, she anticipated no trouble in supporting both herself and the baby.

Her dreams were filled with images of a child—tall, straight, and healthy. He would be a miniature of his father, with a dark headful of hair such as she might have imagined Sloane's to have been in his youth. With every dream her love grew, now given the outlet that Sloane's emotional estrangement had denied her. She had presented him with her terms, and he had rejected them. Here in her womb was one who would not. If Sloane's devotion was to be beyond her reach, she would find it in his child.

The thought of motherhood grew more appealing with each passing day. Indeed, everything seemed to be working out to her satisfaction—until the day of departure arrived and Sloane escorted her aboard the Lear jet used exclusively by his corporation.

"Where are Jerry and Bob?" she asked, seeing neither of

the subexecutives whom Sloane had designated as part of this exploratory team.

He spoke quietly with the pilot before turning to face her. "They'll be meeting us in Juneau. We're making a slight detour."

"Detour? To where?" Suspicion widened her eyes, giving her the look of a lost child. In her deliberate attempt to avoid a weight gain, she had somehow managed to lose several pounds. Her cheeks were more finely sculpted now, her arms and legs even more slender. The overall effect was not displeasing; rather, it gave her an air of studied maturity, becoming in a sophisticated way.

Sloane looked down on her indulgently. "Don't be alarmed. We're stopping in Atlanta for a late lunch, then we'll move on to St. Louis for the night. We'll catch the others tomorrow evening."

The faint pallor which crept up beneath the blusher on her cheeks illustrated the sense of foreboding which suddenly assailed her. Justine felt cornered once more by this man. As the momentary terror at the thought of what she had, knowingly or not, let herself in for surged through her, she swallowed hard. "Is it a business lunch . . . in Atlanta?" She knew the answer even before Sloane confirmed it.

"No." He spoke without hint of emotion. "We're having lunch with my parents at their home."

"Sloane! How could you!" she exclaimed impulsively, then caught herself as quickly, lowering her voice. The hum of the plane's engine and the sensation of movement told her it was too late for escape; exerting her utmost self-control, she willed herself to calmness. "Why didn't you warn me, Sloane?"

"I told you to wear a comfortable traveling dress, didn't I? What other preparation do you need?"

Looking down at the soft fabric of her pale blue sundress and the length of slender leg which stretched from hem to stylishly tan high-heeled sandals, she knew that her appearance would be the least of her worries. Stomach churning, she regarded Sloane again.

"What do they know about me?"

"Only that you are a lawyer and that you'll be accompanying me to Alaska." The rock hardness of his dark eyes was not hidden behind the studied relaxation of his face. Justine felt less than assured—until his eyes suddenly softened. "Take it easy, Justine. It won't be all that bad. They won't bite, you know!"

If only they *had* bitten, she was to rue later, things might have been easier to accept. As it turned out, Justine felt herself drawn to Sloane's parents with a force comparable in strength, though different in nature, to that by which she had been drawn to their son from the start. James and Constance Harper exuded a warmth with every word and gesture—from their presence at the airport in Atlanta to greet the plane, to their vibrant chatter in the car along the route to their house, to the gracious intimacy of the house itself—a Georgian colonial decorated with taste and care—to the informality of the lunch which was eaten on an open patio overlooking lush orchards, to the send-off they gave Sloane and Justine, back at the airport, with heartfelt embraces all around.

In the airplane again, Justine found herself strangely sad. The tarmac blurred beneath the landing gear, and as the craft moved into position for takeoff, her cheeks were wet with tears.

"Are you all right, Justine?" Sloane's arrival from the cockpit startled her. "Has something upset you?"

Quickly she looked away, her feelings all too open, her heart all too vulnerable. "No," she forced herself to whisper, then paused. "They're lovely people, Sloane. I enjoyed meeting them. I can understand why your childhood was such a happy one. They love each other very much." Her mind replayed the small, nearly missed gestures of affection that had passed between the senior Harpers—the clasp of hands, the meeting of eyes, the quiet exchange of smiles, the shared pride in their son. Was that what it could be like?

"That they do, Justine. They may not have the physical energy they once had, but they are very much in love." He settled into a seat near her and fastened his seat belt moments before the plane left the ground.

Justine's head was turned away, her eyes glued to the window. In those few short hours they'd spent in Atlanta, James and Constance Harper had touched her. Now, she felt the loss—a loss she never dreamed she might feel. Against her every effort tears slid, one by one, down the softness of her cheeks. Loneliness overwhelmed her; guilt at the deception she'd practiced drove her deeper into her seat. As grandparents the Harpers would have undoubtedly offered a boundless love. Was it fair to deprive them of what would be a great joy to them? Was life fair?

Sloane's gentle voice broke into her daze, close and filled with concern. "What is it, sweetheart?" His use of the endearment hastened the flow of her tears, until his strong fingers reached out to brush them from her cheeks. "Was it that upsetting for you—meeting my parents?"

The fist at her mouth bore the brunt of teeth which dug mercilessly into it in a vain attempt to staunch the tears. Slowly, she removed it. "It's strange," she began falteringly. "I feel as though I'm leaving old friends. . . ."

"You could see them again . . ." His words died with the suggestion of the future. Breath caught in her throat, she waited for him to finish. *If you marry me.* Wasn't that the logical conclusion? But she couldn't marry him. She wouldn't marry him. And she would never see James and Constance Harper again.

Sloane did not finish the thought. Rather, he took her hand in his and held it for long moments—silently, with neither apology nor explanation—before finally releasing it to sort through some papers.

Exhausted by the accumulation of excitement, apprehension, and pure work that had preceded this trip, Justine slept most of the way to St. Louis. It was, therefore, no wonder that sleep eluded her for much of the night. Nor did it help that Sloane had taken adjacent rooms at the hotel—adjacent and *connecting* rooms. Through much of the night her eye held the door to that room, *his* room. Her mind conjured images of his walking boldly through the door, forcing her to come to terms with the overwhelming attraction that existed between them. But the doorknob was still, with nary a turn. What would she have done had he chosen to enter, she asked herself? All reason dictated a physical distance throughout the trip. After all, their relation-ship had nowhere to go, she mused, given the stalemate on the issue of marriage. And what if he detected some minute change in her body and suspected that she might be carrying his child? That in itself was reason enough to avoid intimacy.

Yet, her eyes lingered on the wide wooden door that sepa-rated her body from his. She imagined his limbs, strong and muscled as she knew them to be, flexed in repose atop the king-sized bed. His flesh would be firm, much of it lightly covered by the dark hair that had never failed to thrill her with its over-whelmingly masculine texture. His face would be peaceful, his features at rest. And the thick thatch of silver-sheened hair would fall across his forehead, just waiting for slender fingers to smooth it aside.

Such were the dreams by which her night was disturbed. They were dreams filled with beauty, desire, ecstasy—as they were nightmares of anguish, frustration, torment. And, all the while, her owl-eyes watched, waiting and wondering, hoping and fearing, planning and imagining—and filled with no small amount of self-reproach at her susceptibility.

The next morning saw the private jet airborne once more, headed for Juneau and the start of the Alaskan expedition. Though Justine had read background material on the state, its topography, and its economy, she was unprepared for the sense of adventure which surged through her at the sight of the landscape below, as the gradual descent over the south-eastern section of the state began. Forgotten were the moments of dismay, disbelief, and apprehension which had preceded the trip. The only reality now was the exhilaration of travel, the joy of visiting new worlds, the excitement of the legal challenge before her.

Alaska—the last frontier of America. Gasping sharply as she looked beyond the steel-bodied jet, she knew it to be true. For, far below, spread with awesome strength over dark, cold bays and inlets and their steep-banked forests of rich green trees were huge, white fingers of ice, gripping the land tenaciously as they had for eons, declaring for all to see that there was, indeed, a greater force than man.

Juneau, the state capital, was a mere breath away from these glacier fields, as every major population center in the state was merely an outskirt of the wilderness. "There are no roads connecting the towns and cities, here," Sloane explained, leaning over to point at the myriad of islands which dotted the coastal approach to Juneau. "Transportation is by ferry—or, of course, by air. This is one of the situations we will be discussing with legislators and labor leaders." His cheek moved against her hair as he moved back, then he straightened and went forward to consult with the pilot, leaving Justine to admire the panorama of jagged mountaintops slashed in turn by picturesque fjords which grew more and more distinct as the plane descended.

Then, with a slowing, a landing, and a light but abrupt stop, they arrived.

So began the adventure. Yet it was unlike anything she had steeled herself to expect. It was as though, with their change of clothes from the light cottons of the New York summer to the heavier wools and denims of the Alaskan fall, they shed the identity of those they had been back east. In truth, there was simply no time to recall those other times, those other heartaches, that very love which had blossomed so quickly that spring.

Rather, Justine found herself thrust into the center of a whirlwind of activity. If she had worried that Sloane's presence would be a torment to her, her fears were unfounded. There was simply no time for torment, with each day crammed from morning to night with meetings and tours, tours and meetings, in endless repetition.

It began in Juneau with several days of meetings with state legislators and representatives of, the governor's office, which was sponsoring the project. Transportation was, indeed, an issue to be worked over, with illustrative ferry tours through the labyrinth of islands. Justine saw firsthand the massive glacial walls of blue and white, heard first hand the moaning and grumbling as the ice shifted, trembled first hand as a glacier calved, sending a monstrous chunk of ice with thundering echo into the ice-cold water. Sloane's hand was warm on her shoulder, his arm absorbing her mirroring tremors. Yet the sight of nature before her held her spellbound.

The group from CORE International visited fishing villages along the coast, inspected large catches of shrimp, trout, salmon, king crab, and halibut, sat sequestered for long hours with fishermen whose fear of oil spill damage, potentially devastating to their livelihood, had reached epidemic proportion.

They surveyed the lumbering country, where mountainous

stands of Sitka spruce, western hemlock, and yellow cedar promised a renewable source of revenue with appropriate planning. They walked through meadows decked with wild flowers, bordering on the glaciers, and spoke with the natives, admiring a culture that demanded preservation.

They boated through bays in the Gulf of Alaska, where Justine was awed by the free soundings of the humpback whales, the lively play of the porpoises, the leisurely romp of the sea lions. She craned her neck to see the eagle, wild and free, soaring to safe haven along the tree-lined coast. And the beauty of the land was brought home to her, laying the groundwork on which the rest of the trip would elaborate. Through it all Sloane was engrossed in deep thought, as was she—their common purpose uniting them, their ultimate goal becoming preservation of the land and its people.

Anchorage came as a surprise to her, fast on the heels of the ruggedness of this southeasterly coast of Alaska. For it was a burgeoning metropolis, the trade center for nearly two-thirds of the state's meager population. With Sloane beside her, she was led down streets bearing signposts identical to many she had seen in New York—on a modified scale, perhaps, but cosmopolitan nonetheless. Bordered on three sides by mountains, the skyline of the city stretched ever upward in futile competition with the grandeur of the wilderness. It was here that Sloane and his crew met with civic leaders in discussions on utilization of the natural resources of coal, lumber, and fresh water to provide a long-range source of work and improved services to the residents of Alaska. As had become her pattern, Justine scrawled notes on her pad during these daytime meetings, then rewrote her thoughts in far greater detail at night in the privacy of her room in the few moments left to her before exhaustion took over, rendering her helplessly and speedily asleep.

From Anchorage the group moved west to the Alaskan peninsula, touring the predominantly mountainous and tree-less islands before spending several days on one of the largest, Kodiak Island. Once again the fishing industry became their primary focus, as they interviewed seamen of both Russian and Scandinavian descent as well as the many native Aleuts who worked out of the bustling harbor. The fears were all the same—the harsh and moody waters of the Gulf of Alaska, the ever-present possibility of natural disaster such as earthquake or volcano, and, with the more recent advent of the trans-Alaska pipeline, the chance of oil spill and its resultant havoc. But there was ever hope and an open ear for new commercial ventures—such as fish canneries and oceanographic farming—to stabilize the economy which, though booming now, was sure to plunge in time.

The lack of the most basic services and dire need of even the most primitive of facilities was never more clear, however, than when they left the milder climate behind and ventured farther north toward the arctic circle and the scattered villages which struggled for survival in a climate at best a challenge, at worst grossly hostile. Justine pulled her down parka in closer to her ears as the tour took them down streets of villages such as Nome, Barrow, and Wainwright. The wind painted bright red burns on her cheeks; her toes threatened to chill forever despite her heavy wool socks and sturdy insulated boots. Yet the Eskimo children ran warmly about, oblivious to the absence of acceptable facili-ties for which their parents now fought. Plumbing, electricity, telecommunications, medical facilities, stores, schools—all were on the list. To these natives Justine's heart went out. Her hand penned note after note of program possibilities and the legislation that would be necessary to set it all in motion.

And then they visited Prudhoe Bay, site of the start of the oil pipeline and, similarly, the boon to Alaska's coffers. The tundra was golden-red with the arctic fall, its wildlife activity in marked contrast to the static mechanical monstrosity of the oil-filled tunnels themselves. Lemmings and ground squirrels scurried about, dwarfed by the caribou which seemed to have accepted the pipeline with characteristic grace. It was a contradictory scene, in Justine's eyes, one which puzzled her throughout the flight back south to Fairbanks.

"Now you understand the fine line we tread in all of this." Sloane spoke softly with her as the plane winged high over mountains unnamed and unscaled. "There is nature . . . and there is *human* nature. The former is precious and should not be disrupted; the latter must push on to survive. The oil pipeline has, aside from its overall appearance, managed to satisfy both elements, though its effect on the environment is a long-range and very tenuous thing."

As he talked on, Justine admired his dedication, the innate intelligence she had seen in action during each and every stop they had made. Now, as they headed for their last, with little over a week left of the trip, he showed no sign of the fatigue which, when she permitted herself to recognize it, had built and compounded itself within her. Perhaps it was a blessing—this all-pervading exhaustion that hit her every night. There had not been a repeat of that soul-destroying craving that had rendered her sleepless that first night in St. Louis. And Sloane had been there, no more than a door or two down the hall each night. Silent congratulations were given and received on the strength of her willpower in steeling herself against him as a man. She prayed it would continue.

Fairbanks was quite different from the other stops on their itinerary. There was a ruggedness about it, a feeling of frontier reality that, even amid her exhaustion, Justine appreciated.

Set at the heart of the great Alaska interior, it was a land of extremes—of heat in summer and cold in winter, of majestic mountain peaks and deep-hollowed valleys. It was a land of the white spruce, the American aspen, the paper birch, and the mountain alder, now painting an early fall splash of copper, gold, and red across the wide, rolling uplands. It was here that the four from CORE International met with representatives of the space communication center, the military, and a delegation from the university, whose environmental studies had veered toward developing industry in agriculture and aquaculture. Again Sloane led the discussions with the utmost of ease and ability, listening for stretches, then directing questions to one member of the hosting group or another. Again Justine admired his command, of himself and of others; again she filled her legal pad with notes regarding the appropriate legal channels for one project or another. She was, above all, determined to do her best, inspired as she was by her leader.

It was following three days of meetings and local expeditions that Justine felt she could go no further. Her mind was saturated with a glut of ideas; her body was plainly drained of energy.

"I've got to get some rest." She took Sloane aside late in the afternoon. "I'm exhausted. Would you mind if I skipped dinner and stayed in my room?"

It had become a common habit for the four to discuss the day's outing over the evening meal, then continue further discussions, some of which lasted for several hours, over coffee. On this particular evening she could barely hold her head up. Faithfully, she had taken the vitamin pills prescribed by her doctor; carefully, she had chosen her diet for the greatest nutritional value. Yet she had been on the go steadily, with no break, for over three weeks.

Sloane studied her weary eyes closely. "Do you think you're coming down with something?" he asked, frowning.

"No. I really need a good night's rest. That's all. Will it be a problem?"

"Of course not. But you should eat. Would you like me to bring you something? Better still," he went on without giving her time to respond, "why don't you go up now. I'll bring something—I'll surprise you—later."

If there was a hint of mischief or, worse, seduction in his tone, Justine was too tired to pay it heed. "Thanks, Sloane," she whispered, laying a tired hand on his arm, then heading for her room.

This hotel was clean and modern, as some of the places they'd stayed had not been. A hot bath on this night was a true luxury, one which she savored for many long minutes. Buoyed by the steaming water, her muscles slowly relaxed; a gentle lethargy seeped through her veins, casting out the intensity of the past weeks, fostering a momentary sense of well-being. It was only when her head nodded, then nodded again, that she finally climbed from the tub, toweled herself dry, and drew her long flannel nightgown over the damp brandy-hued curls to fall softly about her sweet-smelling length. Sleep came instantly, deep and dreamless. She heard no sound; she stirred at no movement. She was mindless of all but the presence of the warm and comfortable cocoon which sheltered her through the night.

It took her several moments to identify the pressure on her shoulder as a hand, several more to drag herself from the depth of slumber to which one part of her stubbornly clung. "Hmmm?" she murmured, opening one eye to make out the lean form of Sloane sitting on the edge of her bed. "Oh, Sloane . . . I fell asleep . . . I forgot . . . all about the dinner you were going to bring . . ."

The hearty laugh which met her ears brought her more fully awake. As her grogginess slowly cleared, she made out a face rested and relaxed, fresh-shaven and in definite good humor. "Oh, I brought the dinner, all right, but you were dead to the world. It's morning now, sweetheart! Time to get up!"

Moaning, she turned away from him. "Let me go back to sleep. I could use two more full days in this bed."

Sloane placed one strong hand on the far side of her so that his arms straddled her, effectively imprisoning her. Puzzled at the sudden aggressiveness, after days, even weeks, of well-tempered propriety on his part, Justine rolled onto her back once more and stared up at him. There was something different in his gaze, a greater relaxation than he had shown since they'd left New York. "If you don't get up soon, I'll be tempted to climb in there with you."

"You wouldn't . . ." she gasped, disguising her true apprehension beneath a veneer of mock horror.

"No, I wouldn't. We have one last flight to take. Jerry and Bob will be leaving for the lower forty-eight in about—" he glanced down at the wide gold-banded watch which contrasted boldly with the bronzed sheen of his skin, "—thirty minutes."

Her rounding eyes threw off the last of the drowsiness. "But I can't be ready in thirty minutes—"

"Shhh. You don't have to be. You and I have our *own* last flight. There's something else I want you to experience . . . before we go back home." His gaze held intensity and humor, plus something else she refused to acknowledge after these many long days.

"What is it, Sloane?" she asked suspiciously.

But he was up and off the bed, headed for the door before she could pin him down more closely. "You'll see. How soon can you be dressed and packed? Just an overnight bag—we'll be back tomorrow. And you'll have to have a good breakfast, considering your lack of dinner last night. Say—an hour—in the lobby?"

"That's . . . fine . . ." she murmured to the emptiness, as he vanished as suddenly as he had entered into her dream world. "Fine," she repeated in a grumble, instinctively wary of what he had in mind, praying that this might be the last challenge to her peace of mind before they returned to New York and could go their separate ways. Even as she thought it, a pang shot through her at the prospect of the trip's end. Much as she wished it weren't so, the proximity to him over the past weeks had been strangely gratifying. As a person he had come to impress her as much as he had as a lover. If nothing else it had been a valuable experience to work with him, to see how a great mind operated in the very broad sphere of his successful business. If only things had been different . . . in him . . . in herself. But they weren't, and she had to accept that. There would be those few interspersed meetings after the return to New York; then he would be gone from her life forever.

Justine went through the motions of washing, dressing, and packing her things, then headed for the coffee shop. As far as pregnancies were reputed to go, this one, she mused, had been relatively easy. She was tired and occasionally queasy, she mused, looking with dismay at the English muffin which soon sat before her, but she hadn't gained weight yet—a blessing, given her precarious situation. Only a week at most to go—and then her worries on that score would be lessened. Constant scrutiny was the danger; once back in New York, Sloane would have less occasion for such scrutiny.

"Did you eat?" Sloane asked first thing when she approached him moments later in the lobby.

"Uh-huh," she lied calmly, uncaring of the deception as long as the coffee itself remained in place in her stomach.

"Then, let's go." Taking her overnight bag easily under one arm and hoisting his own with that hand, he guided her from the hotel to a waiting cab. Before long the airport runway stretched before them. But, to her dismay, rather than being escorted to the jet which had become her second home, Sloane led her to a small, primitive-looking craft, decked with propellers and skis. "A float plane," he explained at her look of bewilderment. "And this is Gus. Gus . . . Justine." He made the introductions, placing her firmly before the burly, bearded form of one Gus Llewellyn. "Gus is a bush pilot . . . one of the best, I'm told."

"You're told right, my friend!" the gruff-voiced giant declared, hefting the luggage into the small rear section of the plane, then lending his hand to hoist Justine up. "There's many that've gone up and come down before their time. I may be a little late getting places on occasion—but I always get there. You can bet on it!"

Stowed safely behind the pilot, Justine threw Sloane a look of helplessness, her eyes rounded in a what-have-you-gotten-me-into-now look. His grin, however, belied any nervousness on his part; indeed, he seemed geared for adventure.

"You like this, don't you, Sloane!" Her accusation, shouted to carry over the chug of the engine, only broadened his smile. His boyishly endearing enthusiasm caused a flip-flop within her; for an instant, she thought of the baby—then realized that the baby had nothing to do with *this* tremor. Chagrin deepened her frown.

"I love it!" Sloane called back from his perch beside the pilot. "This is what I've been waiting for since we arrived. Cheer up! You're in for a treat!"

Her soft-grumbled "Hmmph!" was lost in the din of the takeoff. Skeptical, she turned to watch the progress of the flight.

Sloane's promise had not been an empty one. As Fairbanks fell behind and the craft headed south, the grandeur of Alaska stretched before them in all its awesome beauty. It was an endless jigsaw that materialized as they gained altitude, a meld of golds and greens, blues and grays, a striking juxtaposition of grass and trees, mountains and lakes, all held together by the winding thread of rivers, peaceful before winter's onslaught. Forest growth was more sparse here, with sprinklings of trees in banded clusters, pricking the earth with their shaded quills of evergreen, spruce, and birch.

Above all, in every sense, was the Mountain, ever present, ever closer, yet seemingly ever miles away. "Mount McKinley," Sloane called back to her. "*Denali,* the Indians called it—'the High One.' The highest peak in North America."

Set among a throng of lesser, subservient, yet nonetheless majestic peaks, Mount McKinley stood tall and proud. Its snow-clad slopes blanketed all sound, lending it an air of quiet dignity. Breaths of haze played among its layered subpeaks, seeming to circle but never quite touch the magnificent statesman himself.

Justine sat, breathless, held in the power of the High One, as the plane approached, circled its peak, then continued on its southward course. "What a sight!" she exhaled slowly, drinking it all in with helpless excitement. "Would you want to climb it?" Her forefinger poked, half-playfully, at Sloane to get his attention, but she read the answer in his face, turned toward the granite god. He didn't bother to speak; words were superfluous.

The plane began its descent, carving its airspace through chilling walls of ice. For a minute's mind-play, Justine recalled the concrete peaks of New York City, its avenues the corridors through high-rising blinders. Gradually, the mountains opened though, returning her to this final frontier, spewing the float plane out above a verdant vista. The surface rose to meet them, slowly, then more quickly. With bounces and jolts the skis touched the water, skidding across its surface to a planked dock on the far side of the lake.

What followed was a brief flurry of activity into which Justine was swept unquestioningly, much as had been the case during the earlier part of the trip. She and Sloane disembarked, then retrieved their bags and a number of cartons and crates which Gus automatically passed from the storage hold of the craft. There was no time to look around, to identify the community into which they had just come. Nor was there time for Justine to ponder the absence of a welcome party, as had been the case in all of those other stops. Before she could straighten from lowering the last of the bundles, Gus returned to the cockpit, set off from the dock, taxied across the water, and was airborne.

"Let's go, Justine. We might as well get these things into the cabin."

"The cabin? Where is—" For the first time she turned to study their point of deposit, taking in the wealth of greenery, low-growing ferns, taller grasses, and high-rising trees which inhabited the shore. There, set into its midst, was, indeed, a cabin. Nestled snugly amid the timber was a small log structure, a seeming offshoot of nature itself. "That's the cabin? Where are the others? Where are the people?"

"There aren't any." His words hit her with a force close in intensity to that of the mountains now high in the distance. Without further explanation he bent to lift several boxes and left her to follow. Which she did. Empty-armed. Horrified.

"No people? What is this, Sloane? Why are we here?" Her legs scrambled to keep pace with his, her pulse racing even faster.

"We're here for several days of . . . solitude. Meditation, if you will. Rest, no doubt. Which you need." His pointed glance was apt reminder of her reluctant awakening this morning.

"You didn't say that we'd be in total isolation! I can't stay here!" Her thoughts were of the majesty, not of the mountains now, but of the tall, rugged man beside her.

"You can't leave. There's nowhere to go." Undaunted, his face bore a hint of subtle amusement as he continued his trek.

"Well"—she stopped, placing both hands on her hips—"you can just get that pilot back here to pick me up. I refuse to stay here."

Having reached the steps to the cabin, Sloane placed the boxes on the front porch, fished into a pocket for the key to the large padlock which held the door shut, and shouldered it open. "After you . . ." His large hand gestured for her to precede him into the structure. When she refused to move, but stood, staring open-eyed at him, he shrugged, winked mischievously, and turned to lift the boxes before entering.

Fury surged through her. Trembling, she turned and stormed back to the dock, sitting down hard upon its weathered planks, waiting for the plane that would not be coming to her rescue. There was movement beside her as Sloane made another trip with supplies, yet she did not turn to watch, ignoring both his strength and his command.

The Silver Fox. Now for the first time, she knew the full meaning of the distinction. Silver he was, with that vital crop of thick silver hair. And sharp he was in the business acumen she had witnessed repeatedly over the past weeks. Now she knew that cunning with regards to her—and she bristled. She had fallen into his trap, had been lulled into a false sense of security by the thorough propriety he had shown toward her during the trip. He had crept up stealthily, taking her by surprise. Now she was his unwitting prey.

Anger seemed her only proof against the awesome sensuality he oozed. Anger would have to guide her through this final ordeal. Scowling at the innocent water, its mirrored surface broken every now and then by the play of the Canadian geese, their raucous calls rallying their forces, she felt that anger begin to dissolve even against her will. Daring to look more closely about her, the sight was as serene and welcoming as any she had seen during the expedition. If this was Alaska, she found herself drawn to it.

"Ready to come in?"

His soft invitation startled her from her self-indulgent musings. He knelt close beside her, his eyes less humorous but warmer, threatening to melt her resistance at once.

"No. No," she stammered. "I'll sit out here for a while."

"I won't gobble you up, if that's what has you worried. I didn't bring you here to impose on you something you don't want."

Gobble you up. John Doucette's faraway words echoed in her mind. "Then, why *did* you bring me here? Honestly."

He shifted to sit more comfortably beside her. "Honestly?" His dark eyes held her brighter green ones, mesmerizing her as they seemed too often to do. "Honestly? I brought you here for the reasons I just mentioned. Plus two others."

She waited, counting on him for the truth. When it came, she wished he had been less truthful.

"I felt that, if you were to understand the lure of Alaska, you should see this. It may help frame some of those very valid proposals you've made along the way." The compliment was beyond her.

"That's the first. And the second?"

"The second," he continued, low and calmly, "is that I wanted to be with you. Alone. It's been difficult spending so much time with you, over the past few weeks, with others constantly around. We had something very good going at one point there. Have you forgotten so quickly?" The hardening of his jaw gave credit to his onetime declarations of love. Would they be repeated?

"No." Her voice was very soft. "I haven't forgotten." Looking down, her eyes grazed her stomach, still flat, yet carrying the evidence of that "something very good."

"Then come back to the cabin with me. I won't pressure you . . . for anything. Let's just relax. We owe ourselves that much. It's been a very rough and busy time for us both."

For the first time she saw the lines of fatigue etched in the grooves by his lips, the faint furrows on his brow. Suddenly, it all came back as though there had never been a marriage proposal, a heart-wrenching refusal, an imposed break from the daily routine of her bustling practice in Manhattan, a long three weeks of constant work, the seed of their union growing inside her about which he must never know. Suddenly, there were only the two of them and the frightening bond which held them together.

What he read in her eyes she would never know. But when he stood, then reached down to help her to her feet, she acquiesced. She was simply without the strength to resist. Arms laden with her pocketbook and overnight bag, she silently walked beside him to the cabin.

Chapter 8

Three open wooden steps led to the porch of the cabin. It was on the second that Justine tripped.

"Aaaahhh!" she cried out as she stumbled forward, ramming her elbow in the process. Though protected by the padding of her thick down parka, she nonetheless felt the impact. Her small overnight bag thudded to the ground, her pocketbook sailed forward, its contents spilling over the porch. "Damn!" she swore beneath her breath.

"Uh-uh. Not ladylike," Sloane chided softly, reaching for her. "Are you hurt?"

Lips drawn taut in frustration, she pulled away, gingerly kneading her elbow as she looked up to scold him. "It's just my funny bone . . . and I'm sure this is only the first of the accidents I'm bound to have in this primitive place." But her annoyance was fast fading. Slowly a sheepish grin stole over her features. "See what you're in for?"

"I can take it." He smirked, putting down his own things to help her gather hers. "I'll just have to keep a closer eye on you."

Just what she needed, she mused in silent sarcasm, stuffing personal belongings back into her purse. "It's a miracle this hasn't happened before. But then, when there are others around

I do just fine. It must be the bad influence *you* have on me," she quipped puckishly.

"Could be." His comment was a distracted one, his attention caught on something else. "What's this?" Reaching down, he retrieved the plastic bottle containing her vitamins, those her doctor had prescribed and which she had taken, faithfully, every day.

"Vitamins," she barked with undue haste, grabbing the bottle from his hand and stuffing it into her bag and out of sight.

"Do you always take them?"

"Yes." A slight stretch of the truth, she reasoned.

"By prescription?"

"Yes. They are more effective than anything sold over the counter," she explained, mustering every ounce of nonchalance she could find. "As you've seen, I work very hard."

He eyed her skeptically for several moments before retrieving his things and leading the way into the cabin. Before she had even had a chance to look around, he was on his way out once more, ax in hand. "I'm going to chop some wood for the pile. Make yourself at home." There was an undercurrent of tension in his voice, making her infinitely grateful for the moments of privacy he gave her in which she might collect herself and her scattered composure.

Several deep breaths bolstered her, enabling her to look for the first time around the cabin. Moving slowly, her eye perused the large, single room of the structure, absorbing the freestanding wood stove for heat to her left, the similarly footed wood-burning stove for cooking to her right, the rough-hewn table and chairs farther in, the built-in shelves and storage units all about, before finally coming to rest on the bed. One bed. Large. Anchored to the wall with long, steel spikes. Covered with layers of home-styled quilts. Beckoning and foreboding at once.

It was to the bed that her unsure footsteps took her, crossing the wide rust carpet which was intended for warmth. Slowly, she lowered herself, then looked about once more. How would she survive the intimacy of this cabin? Could she love Sloane freely, as every nerve end screamed to do, all the while knowing that, once back in New York, things would never be the same? There was her career, the fact that Sloane would have her in marriage or not at all, and . . . the baby.

For what seemed an eternity, the rhythmic hammer of the ax echoed through the silent wilderness, the closeness of the cabin, and the ache of her heart. Her mind's eye pictured the ripple of muscles beneath the parka he wore, the flex of muscles in his arms as he would raise the ax, drive it downward, then raise it again. Yet, even amid her inner turmoil was the solace, strange but distinct, that Sloane was here to care for her. Rocked by the steady percussive beat, she slowly relaxed.

"There, that should do it for a while." The tall figure burst into the cabin, his hair gleaming with the light behind, his eyes warm and deep. "Do you feel better now?"

"Yes." Suddenly shy, she struggled to find something to say. "Am—am I supposed to be doing something here? I can't just sit and watch you work."

"Why not?"

"Because it's not my way, and you know it, Sloane Harper."

His grin seared its path to her heart as he turned from lowering the wood before the stove and approached. Parka removed, he wore only the wool shirt which clung to his damp chest. Perspiration put a sheen on his nose and forehead, his hair dipped into its moistness. "You could come out and keep me company while I fish for our dinner." He arched an eyebrow in suggestion. "The fresh air would be good for you."

"Hah! I've had more fresh air in the last few weeks than I've had in years. I'm not sure my lungs will be able to adjust to that thing they call air back home."

"All the more reason to enjoy it now. Come on." The tilt of his head seconded the invitation. Justine accepted it.

Moments later she found herself back on the dock, this time in better humor and engrossed in Sloane's deft handling of the rod and bait. "What do we catch?" she asked.

"Depends what's biting today. Could be salmon; more probably rainbow trout. If you look closely, you can see the breaking of the water as they come up to grab at insects. Look."

Her eyes following his finger to the center of the lake, where, indeed, after a few minutes' silent wait, the surface dimpled for a moment, then was still again. "What else should I be on the lookout for?" she asked facetiously. "Snakes? Sea creatures? Wolves?" Her eyes widened. "Bears? Oh, no, Sloane. *You* heard those stories right along with me. There are plenty of bears out here. Do you have a gun?"

His attention did not waver from his work. "There is one, I think, in the cabin, but I have no intention of using it unless we are in dire danger of attack. Most bears are simply curious. If you see one, just freeze and watch. Unless it is a mother with her cub—and the little ones are pretty big by this time of year—you will be in no real danger."

"Very reassuring," she sneered good-naturedly. "My real danger is from you, is that it?"

In place of the smart retort she had expected came a silence, shrouded by Sloane's abrupt tensing. "No, Justine. Your only danger is from yourself and those preconceived notions you've built your life around. I pose no danger to you."

Swallowing convulsively, she looked away. Unbidden came memories of an earlier discussion, one that had prompted the pain and anguish which only the discovery of her pregnancy had alleviated. Perhaps he was right. How simple it would be to give in to him, to agree to a marriage, even knowing how potentially devastating it might be. But, no. She couldn't change her mind.

"If you brought me out here to sermonize, I won't listen," she murmured softly, her eyes glued to the far-off peaks.

His answer was as low. "Then I won't waste my breath. The silence is too lovely to spoil, unless the talk is constructive."

A new thought hit her. "How long *are* we going to be here, Sloane?"

"Gus will be back in three days. If the weather holds. And if his plane keeps flying. As he said, he may be late, but he always makes it."

"You've been here before, haven't you," she asked, wondering why the realization hadn't come to her sooner.

"To this cabin, no. Out there"—his eyes rose to the mountains—"yes. I was part of an expedition that scaled Mount McKinley nearly ten years ago."

"Were you?" Enthusiasm softened her features quickly. "What was it like?"

He thought for a minute, searching for the words to describe the experience. "It was cold and long. It was the most trying thing, physically, that I've ever done. It was also the most exhilarating, the most satisfying, the most climactic. Almost."

"Almost?" Without thinking, she prodded him. "And what was the *most* climactic?"

The hold on his line slackened as he turned intense eyes toward her. "Making love to you, Justine . . . that topped everything."

"Sloane," she moaned, turning her back to him in self-defense. "Why do you say things like that?"

"Because it is true. You wanted the truth, didn't you? Or would you rather I cushion everything I tell you?"

"No, of course not," she whispered softly. "It's just . . . it makes things . . . so difficult."

"Only if you make them so." Propping the fishing line between his knees, he touched her. For what seemed to be the first time in an eternity, his hands closed over her shoulders and brought her back against him, half-turning her in the process. Instinctively, she finished the turn, burying her face against the warm fabric of his shirt, breathing in his scent and its intoxicating freshness.

God, how she had missed just this, she realized with shock. Much as she had put the physical from mind in the all-encompassing demands of the expedition, this was what her body craved. Her arms stole around his back as she hugged him, mindless of all else but his warmth.

"Whoa!" he cried suddenly. "Wait! I've got a bite!" Sure enough, within minutes, a large fish lay fluttering its last bit of life out on the aged wood planks. "Trout! Perfect! We'll dine in style tonight, my dear!" he drawled, infinitely pleased with himself—as, to her surprise, Justine was with him.

They did dine in style that night. The rusticity of the dark log cabin took nothing from the meal of trout, vegetables, and potatoes, the last two from the supplies they had brought. Even the pains of adjusting to the primitive wood stove as a cooking vessel were forgotten with the first sips of wine and the final taste of fresh-brewed coffee.

"Whose cabin is this, anyway?" she asked as, together, they cleaned up later.

"A young couple, originally from Fairbanks, built this several years ago. They are back in the States, visiting with relatives before the winter sets in. They kindly agreed, through an agent, to lend us the use of their home."

"They built it themselves?" she asked, eyeing the low-beamed ceiling, the close-fitted walls.

"Uh-huh. It is a traditional Alaskan trapper's cabin, the same design that has been used for years. It is built snugly to serve as protection against the cold . . . and the mosquitoes."

"I haven't seen any mosquitoes."

"The season, my dear," he crooned softly, his tone at far odds with the topic of discussion. "The mosquitoes are rampant during June and July. It is too cool and dry for them now. We're lucky. The droning can drive one insane, not to mention the welts they raise. Alaskans do things big . . . including their mosquitoes."

Justine laughed easily. "We heard about those mammoth blueberries. Do you think we'll find any here?"

"Could be. The growing season is short, but the sun shines for such long hours during that time that things seem to grow beyond normal limits. We'll go looking tomorrow."

Tomorrow. But, she asked herself, what about tonight? With the last of the meal finished and cleaned, her eye roamed helplessly to the bed. That one, large bed.

"You go on." He read her mind. "I want to sit up awhile and make some notes for myself."

"I—I didn't bring a nightgown," she mumbled, half to herself. "I more or less assumed that I'd have my own room in a hotel. It seemed silly to pack lots of extras." Even to her, the rationalization sounded feeble.

Sloane was unfazed. "I presume you're wearing long johns beneath those jeans and top?" His gaze speared her.

"Y—yes."

"Then wear those. It will be pretty cold before the night is through."

Given all they'd been through together and particularly given the fact that she carried his child within her, modesty seemed ludicrous. Yet, Justine could not get herself to relax.

Sidling uncomfortably toward the bed, she slowly and reluctantly removed her boots, then her heavy denims and her wool sweater. The chill itself hastened her movements at the end, though she was appreciative of Sloane's preoccupation with his papers on the far side of the room. The weight of the quilts fell in welcoming array about her, yet sleep was elusive.

How long she lay, thinking, wondering, imagining, she couldn't tell. Though the sun had stayed late, its glow had now deserted the small, single window at the front of the cabin. The kerosene lamp by which Sloane worked cast an orange luster about him, its warmth a reflection of that which stole through her quivering limbs. Defensively, she turned her back and snuggled into the far corner of the bed. But, while she might deprive her eyes of the sight of him, his image was vivid in her mind, his presence alive in her senses. When his soft footfall and the rustle of clothing heralded his approach, she stiffened, cringing farther from him. It wouldn't work, she told herself. Yielding to him now would accomplish nothing but a renewal of that devastating torment. But was that worse than the agony she suffered, wanting him, needing him, loving him as she did?

The bed yielded beneath his weight. His hand reached for her. "Justine?" His gentle whisper was nearly drowned out by the thudding of her heart. "Justine? Come here."

Had it not been for her telltale quiver, she might have feigned sleep. But he would know, with those dark and cunning eyes that saw through her as no others could. Silently but determinedly, she shook her head.

"Justine . . . it's cold. Let me warm you."

Again, she shook her head. "I'm fine."

"You're shivering."

"I'm not cold."

"That's just my point."

Once more he had cornered her, caught her in a trap of her own making. The fox lay in wait beside her. How could she escape? "Please, don't, Sloane," she begged softly. "Please let me sleep."

"Is that what you really want? You've always been true to your own feelings, Justine. Don't stop now. Is sleep what you really want?"

His question only added to her torment, embodying it, putting it into poignant words. What *did* she want? The night hung heavy, dark and still, as she wrestled with the dilemma. Her mind said one thing, her body another. Tears gathered behind her closed lids as she held off, held off, fighting what must surely be the inevitable. For she wanted Sloane. It was as simple as that.

With a low sob, she turned and covered the inches that separated them, drawn into Sloane's body, against his manly warmth, with an intermingling of arms that locked the union. She was home. At last. It mattered not for how long. All she knew was that she had come home.

Her tears dampened the firm skin of his shoulder as his arms caressed her shuddering form. "Shhh. It's all right, sweetheart. I love you."

"I—I know. I know," she wept softly, clinging to, him with every ounce of strength she possessed.

He held her until her crying ceased, offering himself as a willing pillow for her pale-copper head, as welcome support for her quaking limbs. "Love me, Sloane," she murmured, as the tears dried and her fingers relaxed their grip to travel over the planes of his bare flesh.

Moaning, he gently slid the thermal jersey over her head, crushing her against him, then worshipping her curves, one by one, with his hands, his lips, his tongue. If he noted a greater fullness in her breasts than that attributable to the heat of passion, he made no mention of it. Her body arched against him, warm and demanding, growing more and more aroused as he coaxed her to peaks unimagined.

"I need you, Justine," he groaned thickly, his hands helping her peel the covering from her slender legs. "You can't imagine—"

"I know," she interrupted in a whisper, seizing the opportunity to lead his body to the height of awareness at which she waited. The leanness of his muscles trembled beneath her questing fingers, making his breathing more ragged than before. His arousal was warm and strong, a pulsing requisite to their mutual satisfaction.

At the apex of desire, she welcomed him, receiving him with warmth, enveloping him with warmth, as his own warmth filled her. Together they scaled that peak, groping ever higher toward that star-filled summit, loving onward and upward, locked in the embrace that brought them finally to the pinnacle for a joyous moment of delirium which hung high and free in mindless suspension, before slowly beginning the downward cascade.

His flesh melded with hers as the wonder of it all held them in breathless ecstasy. Then, as their tremors eased, he shifted to lie beside her, holding her firmly against him. "McKinley pales in comparison, doesn't it?" he gasped, his lips warm against her closed eyes.

"Ummmm." Words could not express the pleasure he had given her, any more than could the life's-beat of her heart so close to his. As they had shared the height of rapture, so they shared the haven of sleep which stole over them. Only the lonely hoot of the horned owl and the anguished howl of the lone wolf broke through the stillness of the night—but they were oblivious to it all. Their only reality was the warmth of each other, and they slept.

Morning brought the feather-softness of warm lips against Justine's eyes. Slowly, she opened them, startled, then eased as the events of yesterday surged back in divine detail. A lazy smile curved the corners of her lips. "Good morning," she whispered. "What time is it?"

"Somewhere in the vicinity of ten. How did you sleep?" His voice was soft and low by her ear. Instinctively, she turned her head toward it.

"Ten? It's late! Shouldn't we—"

A strong finger against her lips stilled her voice. "No, we shouldn't. There's no reason to get up, nothing at all to do. Isn't it lovely?"

Her grin was a mirror of his own. "It is." What was even more lovely was the length of hair-roughened leg that wound between her own smoother limbs. Her curls fell across his chest as she rested her cheek next to his heart. "You lied to me, Sloane."

"Oh? When have I ever lied?"

"You told me, that first day I met you, that you talked in your sleep. I've spent three nights with you now, and I haven't once heard you talk."

"You wear me out. What strength have I got to talk, much less dream. Or"—he paused, a trace of mischief in his voice—"perhaps it's you who is worn out. Perhaps I do talk, but you sleep through it all."

"No way! I'm not that used to sleeping with someone that I'd miss something like that. So I'm not to learn the business secrets?"

"You already know most of them, sweetheart." His arms settled around her, drawing her more comfortably against his body. "And I doubt that there's much that that sharp legal mind of yours misses, anyway."

"You'd be surprised," she murmured, half to herself, thinking of how fully she'd missed the cunning approach he'd taken to her seduction. Not that she'd minded it in the end; last night had been worth every second. Even now, in hindsight, the stirring of desire was not far away. "So"—she cleared her throat of its thickness—"what do we do today?" Angling her head up, she propped her chin on his chest, resting her forearms across its sinewed breadth.

Sloane regarded the low-slung rafters as he listed off the possibilities. "We could walk in the woods, paddle around the lake in the canoe that's out back, hunt for berries . . ."

His voice fell victim to a lazy amusement as he looked down at her, then shifted her onto her side and turned to face her. "What will it be?" he crooned, gently brushing a wispy red curl from her brow, then letting his hands fall lower onto her body.

"I'd like to go berry picking," she began, then sharply sucked in her breath at the riot caused by his wandering touch. "It's an idyllic thought . . . romantic. We could . . . walk through the woods . . . in . . . the bright sunlight . . ."—she draped her leg over his, her breath coming in ever shorter gasps—"hand in hand . . . Adam . . . and Eve . . ."

"It's cold out there," he rasped, needing her.

"We could . . . get . . . dressed . . . aaahh . . . very . . . warmly"— she gasped again as he filled her—"and . . . then . . . bake a . . . pie . . . with . . . the . . . ooooh, Sloane . . ." He moved inside her, warm and throbbing, driving the train of thought from her mind. "You feel so good . . ."

They were silent for a long time, their mouths occupied in the more crucial acts of kissing and exploring, finding new places and deeper secrets. If Justine had thought McKinley to be awesome, the new peak they scaled was no less than mind-boggling, both in its height and its reverence. Long after, they lay in limb-mingled stupor, savoring the beauty of the act and its underlying emotion. It was nearly noon before they stirred again.

The morning's mist had long since risen from the lake when they ventured out to walk, to enjoy nature's splendor. Through the eyes of lovers, the world was that much more spectacular. All thoughts of the Outside were pushed into oblivion in favor of the time they both knew was precious.

Underbrush brittle in the early fall's chill crunched beneath the soles of their boots. The air was white at every exhalation. Justine could now fully appreciate the clothing that Sloane had suggested she wear, for the layered garments were utterly necessary against the cold.

"It's hard to believe that this is still August." She pulled her collar more tightly around her neck. "Is there any real summer here?"

Sloane took her hand, tucking it within his, then into the pocket of his parka. "In June and July, when the sun shines for twenty hours of the day, it can get pretty warm—well into the sixties. But when you stop to consider how close we are to the arctic circle, when you think of those glaciers farther south and look at that snow on the mountains over there, sixty degrees sounds very warm."

The High One, toward which his eye gravitated, was reflected in perfection on the surface of the lake. Her mind made a photograph of the majestic scene—the peaks, the trees, the ferns, the lake, then the twin image in reverse below. As they walked on, there were other sights, many as exciting to store in memory.

There were cranberry bushes approaching their bright red autumn hue, their fragrance creating a luxuriant bouquet. There were the trees, hovering high overhead, much taller now above them than when dwarfed by the mountains. There were the sounds of the wild forest—the flight of the ground squirrel, the twitter of the birds, the rustle of the leaves as a cool breeze stirred up to play in their midst.

"It's all so fresh and untouched," Justine whispered, reluctant to impose the sounds of humanity on the natural bounty.

"That's precisely what has drawn so many people up here from the lower forty-eight." Sloane's appreciation was no less than hers, though he had seen it all before. "They come in search of adventure, of purity and simplicity. Unfortunately, many find themselves in even worse straits once they get here."

Justine recalled some of the bush villages they had visited. "It must be very different to live here year round than just drop in for a short time, as we are doing."

"The rugged ones survive," he spoke his thoughts aloud. "Others are forced to become rugged if they hope to survive. Still others admit failure and either return home or migrate to the cities. The rates of alcoholism and suicide are appalling."

"That's precisely why legislation is needed for programs to deal with it." Justine had made voluminous notes on the topic, based on things they'd seen and learned in the past three weeks. "Is there any hope of passing such legislation? It's one thing to propose it, to point out the problem, but there must be a commitment on the part of the government to follow through."

Sloane's gaze held admiration as it warmed her. "It was the government that hired CORE International in the first place. I'm assuming that if they've made the commitment to us, they will be willing to go further. Actually," he continued, leading her back in the direction of the lake, "the government—at least, this present governor—is committed. With money pouring in from the oil pipeline, there should be plenty to fund social service programs such as you have in mind. He would like a legislative commitment before he leaves office. Unfortunately, the windfall has prompted many citizens to spend wildly. That's where we come in. It's our job to make specific recommendations . . . and then hope."

Later that afternoon they returned to the woods carrying containers which soon brimmed with the largest blueberries Justine had ever seen. Even later the cabin was filled with the delicious aroma of freshly baking pie. In this warm and heady haven, the love they shared knew no bounds. As the heat of the oven warmed the air, their passion sparked, flared, then exploded in a cataclysmic lovemaking that left Justine trembling in awe. How each joining could take her higher than all others before she couldn't imagine. Yet Sloane knew the ways of love and his lessons were endless.

"How can a lawyer be such a good cook?" he asked later, their lips moistly blue from the goodies on which they'd feasted.

"How can a sleeptalker be such a good lover?" she teased in return, leaning forward to kiss the last of the sweets from his lips.

And so it went—a bounty of love growing ever larger, ever deeper as one day melded into the next. One early morning found them at the shoreline, admiring the lacy ribbons of ice which the night air had laid there. "Look at those tracks." Sloane had pointed to the moist dirt at the edge of the ice. "Beaver, muskrat, possibly mink. All wandering freely here." One dusky evening found them on the dock, sitting quietly in awe of the moose and her calf feeding on the succulent aquatic vegetation beyond their view beneath the surface of the water.

Their days were filled with quiet adventure, their nights with tender love. When they awoke on the morning of their last day in the cabin, Justine knew a regret she would not have imagined three days before. "I wish we could stay here forever," she whispered against his throat. His pulsepoint raced, as did hers, in the aftermath of a fiercer lovemaking than they'd known yet. It had been as though each had fought for something extra, as though each had known that this might be the last.

"We could come back here every summer," he spoke more solemnly, "if you were my wife."

"Sloane—" she began, only to be interrupted.

"I want you to marry me, Justine. Nothing can change my feelings."

From the far recesses of her mind the subject of marriage sent a chill through her, intruding abruptly on the warmth of the closeness they shared. She remained silent for long moments, as her hands slipped from his chest and she lay back on the bed. When she finally spoke, her voice was hushed.

"It's unfair to discuss this now."

"Why?" Sloane loomed suddenly above her, his dark eyes filled with challenge. "Why shouldn't we discuss it now? These few days should have shown you what it would be like."

"That's exactly it," she argued. "These few days have shown me how much I love you. But these days have been spent in a kind of fantasy. This life, this cabin, these woods aren't the real world as you and I both know it. The real world for us is back in New York, in the city, with our respective work and offices. I've fought a long time to get where I am, Sloane. You have to understand that."

His jaw moved in, tensing. "I'm trying. Believe me, I'm trying. But I'm beginning to lose patience."

"Patience? Is that all it takes to make a marriage work? You may have climbed Mount McKinley, but, from what I've seen, it takes a lot more stamina, a much longer haul to make a marriage work—really work."

"And you're not willing to try?" His lips were thinned, his muscles taut.

"It's not just me to consider," she began, then stopped herself in shock at the confession she'd nearly made. Carefully she chose her words. "I've seen what a poor marriage, even a mediocre one can do to children. And I'm sure you want children." Her green-eyed gaze speared him with undue intensity.

"In time. But that's not the central issue. I will never marry purely for the sake of having children. I want the happiness that would come from spending the rest of my life with the woman I love. And I love you, Justine."

His reasoning was too sure, his words too close to her heart. If she listened any longer, she might well give in. And *that* she could never do. *In time* he might want children. Well, she reminded herself, there was to be one in six short months—not much time to work the bugs out of a new marriage. "I can't," she whispered in misery, scrambling from the bed and searching for her clothes. "You ask too much."

Sloane said nothing, merely lay back on the bed and threw a strong forearm across his eyes. Justine's heart ached in anguish, yet she knew what she must do. Dressing quickly, she dashed outside, fleeing the lair of the Silver Fox. As she sat on the dock, waiting for him to join her with their bags, the war raged on within herself, heart against mind, until her stomach churned. It was only a sharp pain in her side that gave her warning that, if she did not pull herself together, she might lose it all.

Sloane didn't broach the topic again, yet it hung between them as an impenetrable wall. Conversation was light, nearly nonexistent, as the small float plane returned them to Fairbanks, where his private jet awaited them. The long flight to New York seemed even longer this time, though there were no diversionary lunches in Atlanta to slow them. It was only as they circled Kennedy International Airport that Sloane approached her. He looked strangely haggard, considering the pure relaxation they'd indulged in during the past few days. And the air of defeat about him carried only a hint of the pride she'd grown to love.

"I think that I've reached the end of my tether, Justine," he began softly, sitting stiffly beside her in the empty aft cabin of the craft. "You know that I love you and that I want to marry you. If you still refuse me, I would rather we sever the entire relationship."

Her heart lurched; her stomach turned. It was inevitable, yet no easier to accept. Eyes rounded in green-glazed apprehension, she listened.

"It might be better if you gave your notes, your proposals, to another member of the firm. I think that the work would be better accomplished without the tension that would exist between us."

Tears blurred the image of her hands, knotting themselves in her lap. "So I'm to be fired?" she whispered, appalled at her resort to half humor.

"In a word, yes. Your work on this expedition has been exceptional. Let's just call it . . . a difference of opinion. Irreconcilable differences. Is that better? A divorce before the marriage. That's what you've assumed all along, isn't it?"

Justine raised her head to argue, but Sloane's back was to her, long strides taking him forward to the cockpit. Swallowing the knot in her throat, she was less successful with the tears. As the plane touched down on home turf, she knew it was over. Had she planned it all along? Was Sloane right? But she would never know. He had left her himself. It was too late. Placing dark glasses over her eyes, the same ones that had kept the glare of the arctic sun from scorching her, she gathered her things and left the plane, his love, and a future with Sloane—all behind.

Chapter 9

If only her own love, that abiding love she felt for Sloane, were as easily cast off. In the days that followed, Justine was haunted by it. It imprisoned her heart, suffusing her life's blood with torment, loneliness, frustration. It permeated her every activity—followed her to work, then home, to dinner or lunch or sleep. Even the thought of the child she carried was no solace; for, to her surprise, there was still little sign of her pregnancy. She was as slim, perhaps slimmer, than ever; somehow, the pregnancy seemed unreal, a hoax.

The results of her weeks as a member of the CORE International team were dutifully passed on to Phillip Marsh, the lawyer designated as her replacement. Much as she knew that the transfer was for the best, the psychological separation was but one other thorn in her side. In the firm's understanding, thanks to Sloane's diplomacy, she had withdrawn from the case for valid logistical reasons, mostly pertaining to her own work and its demands. None of her colleagues knew the truth.

"Well, Justine," John Doucette welcomed her back to the office when she finally showed up several days after the return from Alaska, "how did it go?"

"Not bad," she murmured, barely looking up from the mountain of papers and messages that had accumulated in her absence.

"Was Sloane the perfect gentleman? A good boss?"

The mention of Sloane's name sent a shaft of anguish into her. "We managed to get a lot done, if that's what you're asking. I believe that the project will make a solid impact on the problems that exist in the state."

As John questioned her for details, she gave them without a fight, feeling too drained emotionally to muster either protest or banter. And, she forced herself to relax; as long as her colleague stuck to the legal issues involved, there was no problem. Unfortunately, he did not. After a few moments of relatively passive conversation, he eyed her speculatively.

"You sound different. As though you left some of that spirit back up there in Alaska." Despite the sudden clenching of her fists, he persisted, voice lowered yet direct. "I did some checking on the arctic fox while you were gone. He's adapted well to his environment, they say. Ears are shorter; less susceptible to frostbite—that type of thing." Justine felt the churning in her stomach begin anew. "And, the arctic fox, it seems, is the mildest, most well behaved, most pleasant of all the wild dogs."

"John"—she broke into his monologue with thick-tongued haste—"would you mind stopping that. It's lost all its humor."

His gaze took in her pallor, the slight quiver of her lips, the haunted cast to her dull emerald orbs. "So have you, Justine. Are you all right?"

Her breathing faltered with a deep inhalation. "I will be," she spoke very softly, "once I get back to this work. The whole pile of it"—she gestured to the mess on her desk, clutching at the most logical change of subject—"has gotten me down."

"If there's anything I can do . . ." For the first time since she'd known him, John seemed truly sympathetic. His sincerity brought a faint smile to her lips.

"I doubt it, John. But . . . thanks for the offer. It's nice to have . . . friends . . . to count on. . . ." Quickly she lowered her eyes to her work, missing the subsequent look of puzzlement which flickered over the other lawyer's features before he finally turned and left her office.

Gaze still downcast, she contemplated his newest gems. *Mildest. Most well behaved. Most pleasant.* All these things Sloane had been during their stay in Alaska. And adapted to the environment—that, too. Her memory groped eagerly at the image of his broad-shouldered frame chopping wood, carting pails of water from the lake, stoking the fire in the old wood stove. Then, with a lower slump of her shoulders, she realized that she would never know this magnificence again—and the familiar pall settled over her. The Silver Fox—how very much she missed him!

With Labor Day come and gone, Justine threw herself head-long into the many cases she'd taken on, the only antidote she could find for her rattled nerves. But what had always worked in the past was now less effective. The addiction had grown too strong, having been built slowly and with gathering strength during the Alaska trip; cold-turkey withdrawal took its toll. Instead of feeling diverted by her work, she merely felt tired. Instead of exhilaration, she knew exhaustion. Instead of gaining strength as the days passed, she grew weaker and less enthusiastic about the law in particular and life in general.

Ten days after her return, she saw her doctor for a regular checkup. Her hopes lay here, in the child within her, in the possibility of hearing a heartbeat, in the need for encouragement that the doctor might provide. The waiting room of the office was filled with other mothers-to-be, each one glowing, each one jubilant in comparison to the lethargy she felt. The doctor took one look at her and confirmed the worst of her fears.

"You look terrible, Justine!" In his early forties, he was a good friend of Susan's from the hospital and the natural choice for Justine to see for the prenatal care of her child. "My God, aren't you sleeping?"

"It's been . . . harder lately. . . ." She avoided direct touch with his gaze, knowing how transparent hers would be. His examination was intimate enough.

"Frankly, I'm concerned about you," he began after his examination when she had dressed and returned to her chair. "You're exhausted. Your blood pressure is low. You've lost weight."

"The baby? Can you hear anything?" It was her only hope for salvation; desperately, she grasped at straws.

"Not yet. And it's not that unusual. If the baby is small, we may not hear any heartbeat for another few weeks. But Justine"—he leaned forward to stress the urgency of his advice—"you've got to take better care of yourself—for the sake of the child, if nothing else. You're taking the vitamins?" She nodded. "Good. Now, I want you to get rest—bed rest—for the next two days."

"But I have to go to work—"

"The work will wait! Someone will have to cover for you. You need to be off your feet. You need to sleep."

A sense of defeat crept through her. Now, she mused, she was to be deprived of even her onetime means of escape. "Shouldn't I be . . . getting . . . fat?" she asked timidly.

"Plump," the doctor corrected gently. "You will. But you have to eat properly. And, I want to see you next week."

"Next week? So soon?" The sharp loden tinge of her eyes mirrored her alarm.

"It's all right, Justine," he quickly soothed her. "I just want to make sure you're following my instructions. And, maybe then

164

we'll hear that heartbeat you've been waiting for." His smile was meant by way of encouragement, hiding a deeper concern. He followed her departing form before lifting the phone.

Justine's return home was met by a very solicitous and particularly officious Susan, who hustled her instantly to bed before setting off for work herself. "Now, I expect to find you here when I get back in the morning," she instructed firmly, disturbed herself by her roommate's lack of resistance. "See you later!"

The patient stayed in bed that night and the whole of the following day, insisting on communicating with the office by phone, dozing only occasionally between calls. Her mind was in a strange void, as though waiting for something to happen. It did. That night. While Susan was at work.

It began slowly, gently at first, with a dull ache in her back. The pains were nothing more than a cramp, and she promptly ignored them. There was, she reasoned irrationally, no way there could be anything wrong with her baby. After all, it was all she had left.

Through the night she refused to admit a problem. By morning, however, the matter was taken out of her hands. "Justine! My God! You're positively ashen!" Susan's trained eye took in her friend's tucked-up position on the couch, the hand that lay weakly on her abdomen. "What is it? Cramps?"

Justine sighed and lay her head back against the upholstery. "It's nothing, Sue. Really. A twinge now and then. I'm sure it's perfectly normal."

But Susan had heard enough. Her hand went instantly to the phone; her voice carried moments later in disjointed phrases to Justine. "Sure, Tom. We'll be there in about . . . twenty minutes." The receiver hit its cradle as the nurse whirled into action. "Come on, hun. We're meeting Tom at the hospital. He's going to take a look at you."

Justine sat up quickly, feeling suddenly faint. "But there's nothing wrong. Honestly. I'm fine."

"You may be a great lawyer"—the determined Susan had disappeared into Justine's room for her clothes—"but you're *no doctor* and a very lousy patient!" Having returned, she stood before Justine. "Now, will you come willingly, or do I call an ambulance?"

Strangely frightened, Justine allowed herself to be led through the motions of dressing, then found herself in a cab with Susan, and, moments later, at the emergency room of the hospital, where they were met by a somberfaced Tom, who whisked Justine off.

For Justine, the world and its happenings took on unreal distortion. It was as though, having admitted to herself the possibility of a problem with the baby, she released a floodgate of activity about her. Nurses and technicians came and went; her doctor stayed with her, examining, probing, questioning. The sedative he administered gave further chimerical quality to the happenings. Few things retained meaning; most shimmered above and beyond her. At the mention of Sloane's name, however, her senses cleared.

"Should I call him, hun?" Susan asked gently as Justine was wheeled toward the elevator that would take her into the deeper womb of the hospital. "He should be here—"

"No!" Her voice seemed distant, foreign. "No! Not Sloane!"

"Is there anyone you want me to call?" The elevator door was about to close as Susan bent over her friend for a last moment.

Justine's whisper was barely audible. "Tony. Tell Tony I'm here."

Tony was beside her, sitting on the edge of her bed when she awoke from a doze that evening. His eyes were warm, despite their concern. "How do you feel?" he murmured softly. The lights in the room, a private one, were dim, creating the restful atmosphere the doctor ordered.

Reorientation was something that had taken Justine time during the late afternoon hours as the anesthesia had worn off. Now she struggled to surface again. "Kind of numb. Empty." Her hand reached out for his, and he offered it, his grip strong and supportive.

"Why didn't you tell me before, Justine? You should have shared this with someone."

The lump in her throat made speaking difficult. After a few minutes' wait, it eased. "Susan knew. I . . . didn't want to . . . burden anyone else."

"Burden? Justine, I'm your brother! If you can't rely on me, who *can* you rely on?"

At that instant Justine knew something she had avoided facing for countless years. Blood *did* flow thicker than water—an old adage, but very true. In the moment of recognition, her eyes filled with tears. "Thanks for . . . being here, Tony." Her voice broke. "I need . . ."

Gently, Tony gathered her into his arms, rocking her trembling form as she wept against him. "I'm here, Justine. I'll always be here." His mind was on another man, as was hers. Through her tears she saw him standing there at the door, tall, straight, silver-haired, and debonair in his finely tailored suit with a trenchcoat thrown over his elbow. But when she blinked, he was gone, a fleeting figment of her strained imagination.

"I wanted the baby so, Tony. You have no idea." With the quieting of her body came the need for release. Her eyes glistened a deep emerald as she unloaded her heart to this person closest, now, to her. "I never thought—or planned—to have children." Her breath hiccuped between words. "But, once it happened, it was as though there was no other way to live."

Again, she thought of Sloane, of his child she would never have. "I feel so . . . alone . . ." Her eyes filled again; Tony let her cry freely.

A counselor by profession, he knew of her need for self-expurgation. "Tell me about the trip," he asked, watching her face light slowly in memory. As her body rested back against the pillows, she talked quietly, telling him everything that had happened since she had seen him last, before her departure for Alaska. Details of the last three days of the trip were unnecessary; the glow in her eyes, suddenly clear and sharp and vital amid the pallor of her skin, elaborated fully. Tony knew enough, however, not to venture into a deeper discussion of Sloane, considering Justine's shaky emotional state. To his dismay the life that had crept into her features during her discourse faded instantly at its end. There was a finality to her silence, a strong depression hovering about her.

"The doctor says you can leave in the morning." He finally urged her to face the future. "I'm going to pick you up at around ten, then I'll take you home and nurse you for the day."

The suggestion brought an unbidden smile to her sober face. "You don't have to do that—"

"I know. But I want to. It's nice to have someone . . . special . . . to take care of."

She clasped his hand as tightly as her siphoned strength would allow. "What *you* need, my brother, is a wife and children."

"I've got time," he retorted with a mischievous smile. "After all, I'm not *quite* as old as you."

His words were meant in jest, yet she looked up with pitiful sorrow at him. "I'm feeling very old right now. I know it's ridiculous—I'm only twenty-nine. But I'm not sure what I want anymore. And it's very disconcerting."

"It's been a bad day for you. Get some sleep," he urged softly, leaning forward to kiss her strawberry-blond crown, "and we'll talk more about it tomorrow."

True to his word, Tony had cleared his day of all commitments, and after seeing Justine comfortably settled and covered on the couch in her living room, he brewed some hot tea and joined her, folding his ample build into the armchair opposite. "There," he declared with satisfaction, combing his fingers through the auburn hair that had fallen across his forehead in the course of his ministrations, "you look better now. Comfortable?"

"Comfortable." Her hand was steadier as she sipped her tea, then looked across at the young man whose features were so very similar to those she had looked at every morning of her life. The comfort of his presence was new to her; instinctively, she wondered about his feelings on the matter. "What are you thinking?" His frown was enigmatic.

"I was thinking how much I would like to see you smile. You look as though you have nothing in life to look forward to . . . and I know for a fact that that isn't true."

The smile she tried to produce was meek. Her night had been filled with thoughts of loneliness and desolation, of remorse and self-doubt, of Sloane and the child she'd lost. "Things look very bleak right about now," she murmured, looking down at the whiteness of her hands against the hunter green of her quilt. "I suppose . . . in time . . ."

"You have to *do it* yourself, Justine. For as long as I've known you, you've never been one to sit back and wait for things to happen. You have to decide what you want . . . then go after it." He hesitated, calculating her strength, then made his judgment. "What about Sloane?"

Nonchalance was impossible; her head shot up. "What about him?"

"Do you still love him?"

"Yes."

"Then *he* should be here with you, not me. Why didn't you have Susan call him from the hospital?"

"He never knew about the baby. I saw no point . . ." Her voice died off as she sought diversion. But it wouldn't come. All thoughts led to Sloane.

"He loves you?" She nodded. "He wants to marry you?"

"He did," she whispered, her gaze searching the room, seeing nothing at all. "I believe he's given up on me now." Tears pricked her lids. "It's for the best. I could never marry him."

"I've asked you this before, Justine," he began, leaning forward in earnestness, "and I'm going to ask you again. Why not?"

"Because . . . it wouldn't work. Marriage doesn't work. If I am temporarily unhappy now, it would be that much worse . . . once the honeymoon was over. It would be like . . . jumping from the frying pan into the fire."

Tony shook his head vigorously. "You're all wrong. You've decided beforehand what it might be like—you've decided beforehand what life, for that matter, is going to be like. You see what you want, Justine. You have selected for viewing only that which reinforces your own beliefs. And you're dead wrong!"

He had her undivided attention, was the recipient of the stunned gaze she held on him. "How can you say that, Tony? *You,* of all people? Weren't you at all affected by your *own* childhood experience?"

"You know very little about that, Justine." With utter solemnity he sat back in his chair, his eyes never leaving hers. "You know, since the first time we met, when my father told me to look you up—remember? You were a junior at Sarah Lawrence; I was a lowly high school sophomore visiting the east for the first time." He smiled wanly at the memory. "From that first time you never asked me about details. I always wondered why."

Sensing that he was on the verge of the truth, she offered her own explanation. "It was none of my business. It wasn't my place to question you."

"No, no, Justine. That was an excuse. You must have wondered. It would have been only natural. Well"—he softened his tone to allow for compassion—"I think you were always afraid to learn that I may have had a very pleasant childhood." He held a hand out to stem her protest. "I don't mean criticism, Justine. I would have done the same myself. It would have been easier to believe that your father—our father—was a bastard."

Her breath came more quickly as Justine listened. She knew it all had to come out, and she hadn't the strength to resist Tony's stark determination. Apprehension held her speechless; unbidden curiosity held her captive of his every word.

"Well, he wasn't. He was—is—a very wonderful person."

"You're prejudiced."

"Yes." He nodded, and she wondered whether Tony was a younger version of that very man under discussion. "But the fact remains that he is a warm and generous and loving man."

"Is that why"—her deep-seated bitterness made an impromptu appearance—"he never contacted me after he and my mother were divorced? Is that why he left me alone, to be shuttled back and forth to the least fortunate relative? Is that why I've been totally on my own since I was eighteen?"

"He was hurt—" Tony began in explanation, only to be interrupted by her cutting cry.

"So was I! Where was he then?" Drained by her outburst, she collapsed against the couch and laid her head back, eyes closed. But she listened; she listened as, with quiet insistence, Tony told the story she had avoided hearing for so long.

"Timothy O'Neill is a very proud man. He had nothing when he met your mother. They talked of things they could build together—with his mind and her money. They never talked of love; it seemed secondary to them. When they married, it was a merger, with each party contributing his share in hopes of a great success. Unfortunately, there was a personality clash early on. Though they lived together as man and wife for a time, they never felt any warmth for each other. *You* were the only worthwhile product of the union."

"How do you know all this? Did my—did *he* tell you?"

"Bit by bit. It was hard for him to talk about it."

"If there were no feelings of love between him and my mother, why was he so disturbed?" she asked skeptically.

Tony's expression was one of reproach. "There was *you*. The marriage itself meant nothing to him. But he did love you."

"Yet he gave me up—lock, stock, and barrel?"

"He had no choice. Your mother saw to that. Look"—he quickly qualified his statement—"I have nothing to say against your mother. It was a mistake they both made. And *he* has had nothing bad to say about your mother . . . ever. Perhaps that was why he waited so long to even discuss it; perhaps he had to understand it himself." He paused, took a deep breath, then continued. "At any rate, the terms of the divorce were that she had sole custody. Your mother left with you and forbid him to come near."

The lawyer in Justine broke forth. "How could any court abide by that kind of decision? He could have sued for visitation rights."

Tony shook his head sadly. "I'm sure you recall how messy the trial itself was. And"—his voice lowered—"the fact that your father had a woman he declared himself in love with *and* . . . an illegitimate son . . . didn't help his cause. That's adultery, among other things."

For the first time Justine thought of the discomfort Tony would be feeling in this retelling of the events of so long ago. With this realization came a gentling of her voice. "Tell me about your childhood. *Was* it a happy one, Tony?"

His smile was nearly apologetic. "Yes. It was. Very happy. I had two parents, each of whom loved me and adored each other. Oh, there were the same minor traumas that all families live with—small illnesses, dubious school grades, inflation. Though we weren't what I would call wealthy, we lived very comfortably. Despite his differences with your mother, Timothy O'Neill was a solid, dependable man."

For long moments of silence Justine ingested his words. If she had feared them, she wasn't now sure why. The picture Tony had painted of his parents and home was a lovely one, a comforting one. Yet, she had never been able to face this possibility before. Why?

"He thought of you often, Justine. Every year, come April second, he would go into his den and sit, alone, thinking."

Justine gasped, her eyes widening and flooding. "My birthday . . ."

"That's right. Your birthday. He was afraid, though. Justine, you have to understand that he was human. And he was afraid. He was afraid that you wouldn't want to see him, after everything that had happened. That was why he sent me." He smiled in remembrance. "When I first saw you, I knew you immediately. Then, I went home. Dad questioned me for hours about you. He wanted to know everything." He sobered once more. "I won't say that he has pined away his life, Justine. That wouldn't be true. He is determined to live life to its fullest—isn't that what we all share?" She nodded as he went on. "But you were never far from his thoughts. You were his own private child. He was— he *is* very proud of you."

173

It was all so difficult for her to absorb that Justine found her cheeks damp once more. For years she had hated her father, had pictured him an ogre for not claiming her. For years she had generalized from her experience to others, refusing to hear, to listen, to stories similar to the one Tony had just told. Confusion was compounded as the intensely caring man across the room spoke again.

"And that's why you are wrong to shut yourself off from Sloane. It's obvious how much you love him, Justine, and, from what you describe of his attempts to keep you near him, he must return that feeling. Your parents were *not* the norm; there was *never* any love there, not even at the start. With you and Sloane, it is different. You would be basing your future on a very strong love and you would have a solid frame on which to work. Oh, I'm not saying," he continued gently, "that there wouldn't be problems. No two people can live, day in, day out with each other without minor differences of opinion. That's what being an individual is all about. But the coming together—it would be there for you and Sloane. You simply have to want it enough. You have to be willing to fight for it—*if* it means enough to you."

Fight for it. His words echoed through her mind in endless reverberation over the next few days. Hadn't she been a fighter—when it came to her education, to her right to go to law school, to her equal opportunity as a lawyer? In those cases she had known the cause for which she fought. But what did she want now? What was she to fight for?

There was no child to fight for; the sinking in of that knowledge left her half-whole and deeply sorrowed. Yet, had she wanted the child for itself or as a mind-link to Sloane? Much as she wanted to believe that the former was true, in good faith she could not. Oh, yes, she had wanted Sloane's child with all her heart; but it was *Sloane's* she wanted, only *Sloane's.*

Days and nights of soul-searching brought things into sharper focus. Analytically she examined what she had. There was her career, on hold now, but waiting impatiently for her return. There were her friends, ever solicitous about her "illness" and a diversionary comfort. There was a future of more work, new friends, perhaps travel—yet it all lacked one essential ingredient.

With the return of her physical strength came the strength to admit that she had been wrong. In all her life's plans, she had never allowed for love. It had taken her by storm. Sloane himself had taken her by storm. Now, the presence of love shaded every other aspect of her life. In the time she had known him, in the times they had spent together, in the very depth of love they had shared, she had known a completeness of her character, a true and utter contentment. Only now that she'd seen what love could do did she see what she had missed before. Only in hindsight did she know the meaning of love. And—in foresight—what then?

Could she agree to marry Sloane and risk an even greater pain than that of going through life without him? As she asked herself this very question, she knew its answer. Its answer was in the ache in her heart, the emptiness in her womb, the deep, deep yearning in the dark-hidden core that cried out for him. For the first time she knew that the pain of facing life without Sloane would be infinitely greater than any other possible source of pain. Therein, her decision was made.

It was nearly three weeks following her miscarriage, an early Wednesday evening. Her time was chosen well, calculating as she had that Sloane would be staying in the city at his penthouse, rather than driving out to Westport.

As she carefully dressed, she felt a spark of life she hadn't felt since before her return from Alaska. It was mid-October now. New York was embroiled in an Indian summer such as it hadn't known in years. Temperatures had hovered in the high eighties for two days; on this evening it was warm but comfortable. Though she had put on several pounds during the past weeks, Justine was aware of the loose fit of her sand-hued gabardine slacks, grateful for the pleats in front and the belt at the waist that, cinched in, gave the fitted look she wanted. Her blouse was of soft brown silk, draped easily over her arms, falling softly from her shoulders and breasts to disappear into her pants. Rest had erased the dark smudges from beneath her eyes, as it had eased the lines of tension which had been present when he had last seen her.

Lightly applying dabs of mascara and blusher, she glossed her lips, fluffed her hair, then stood back, eyeing the woman in the mirror with intent scrutiny. Attractive, yes. Stunning, no. Vulnerable, yes. Confident, no. And very, very apprehensive, without a doubt.

With momentary determination, she cleared her mind of the situations she might face when she finally saw Sloane. She wouldn't take it that far. Every instinct told her that to see him, to talk with him, was imperative, yet what she would say or do was still a mystery to her. Unseen forces drove her on, bidding her gather her purse and keys, take the elevator to the lobby, and slide into the cab which the doorman summoned. It was her voice that issued the address, her hand that fumbled with her wallet as she arrived at her destination, her eyes that spoke of uncertainty as she entered the stately high rise and encountered its security guard.

"Sloane Harper, please," she said, willing calm.

"Is he expecting you?"

"N—no."

"Your name?"

"Justine O'Neill."

With an odd look, the properly attired guard studied her as he mumbled into the mouthpiece of his phone. His expression was hard and impersonal when he faced her directly. "Go on up, Ms. O'Neill. The penthouse."

"I—I know." Lowering her eyes, she moved past him to the elevator, doubt growing with every footfall, every step bringing second thoughts. What was she doing here? Should she turn back? What could she say? Perhaps she should run . . .

Fears nagged at her, confusion assailed her. The elevator skyrocketed her smoothly to the penthouse as her self-possession bottomed out. The door slid open and held for several moments. It had begun its automatic close when she finally stayed it with the touch of her hand. Timidly, she stepped out.

There was one door at the far end of the corridor—a heavy oak-grained door. It was open. Heart lurching, she began the long walk. Slowly, the doorway came ever closer. In the dimness of the inner hallway she could see nothing. It was as though she were being drawn inexorably to the spot, to the man—as it had always been for her with Sloane.

Reaching the door, she stopped. Was it too late to turn? What would he say? Perhaps he would turn her away. Perhaps he would tell her his love had died. Perhaps he would . . . be . . . with another woman . . .

Gathering herself, Justine fought the demon of fear within her. She knew that she wanted Sloane. Yes, she wanted him in every way imaginable. She wanted him as lover, friend, and—yes—husband. And she was prepared to fight!

All was quiet within. Stepping over the threshold, she closed the door behind her. From the small central hallway her eye gravitated to the large living room beyond. It was decorated handsomely with dark Spanish pieces covered in browns, oranges, and creams. Masculinity was all about, yet there was nothing harsh about the room. Its floors bore a thick patterned carpet; its walls offered paintings and prints of the European theme. The far wall was a floor-to-ceiling window. And before it stood Sloane, his back to her, his hands thrust into the pockets of his tailored slacks.

For a brief instant every doubt, every question, converged on Justine, rendering her knees weak, her limbs trembling. But only for an instant. Then something else took over. A surge of strength, born of determination, surged through her. If she had been thought to be effective in the courtroom, this would be her greatest trial. Whether the conversation now proved to be an opening statement or a closing one would depend, in large part, on how she expressed herself in the next few moments. Fists white-knuckled, she took a step forward, then stopped. For Sloane turned around and speared her with a look meant to injure.

"What do you want?" he growled malevolently, eyes narrowed, body in a state of coiled readiness. He was the Silver Fox, ready to attack his wounded prey for the final time.

Chapter 10

It took every ounce of courage she possessed to keep from cowering from him. He was menacing in his anger, devastating in his very evident disdain. And she was his prey, helpless before him, possessing but one source of defense—her love. On it she relied to give her strength.

Sloane's fury assaulted her head-on. "Why have you come?" he seethed. "I thought we settled everything that had to be settled between us. What is it you want now?"

Dressed in dark linen slacks and a light blue sport shirt, open at the neck and rolled at the cuffs, he was compelling. She recalled the first time she had seen him and knew that this was no different. Even in his anger, she was drawn to him.

"We have to talk, Sloane."

"We've already talked. What more is there to say?" The force of his attack nearly crumbled her resolve. Only love kept her going.

"I was wrong," she began softly, then spoke with the conviction she felt. "I was wrong back then. I've made a terrible mistake."

There was neither gloating nor any other outward sign of triumph in Sloane. His glower persisted; her mind conjured up the image of the fox, teeth bared, ears flat back, ready to lunge given that slightest bit of provocation. But provocation was not what she had in mind. Determinedly she went on.

"You were right. I have gone through life with blinders on regarding things such as marriage, children, happiness. I only knew that I was hurt when I was a child and I would do anything to avoid a repeat of that." When he said nothing, but merely stared sharply at her, she wondered if they were beyond the point of reconciliation. Had his love turned to hate so easily? Compulsively, she continued.

"I hadn't planned on falling in love, Sloane. I had dated enough over the years, but things had always petered out before there was any kind of emotional involvement—maybe that's why they did peter out, precisely because of the superficiality of the relationship. When I met you, things were different. Before I even knew what was happening, I was in love with you."

Dropping her gaze, she studied the design underfoot, blindly tracing its bold lines, trying to gather her thoughts into coherent speech. Sloane was obviously going to be no help to her. She was on her own.

"I'm not sure what I expected to happen after that weekend in Westport. I knew that I loved you, yet I believed that I simply couldn't marry you. You have to understand—I've spent a lifetime vowing to remain unattached. Suddenly, you came along. I couldn't change those long-held beliefs overnight."

Sloane had not moved during her argument. There was neither a blink nor a flinch; nor was there sign that he intended to react. Justine's eyes felt the harshness of his gaze; against her will, she began to wilt. If it was all for naught, he should just tell her to leave, that he did not love her as he had once.

Hands twisted convulsively at her waist, she felt she could

say no more without some sign that he was hearing her. "*Say something, Sloane,*" she finally cried.

Despite the bridled anger which held his features taut, his voice was remarkably steady. "Do you love me, Justine?"

Her eyes filled with hope, then flooded with fear. Was he bent on bringing her to her knees, on total humiliation? Well, she decided, tilting her chin higher, if he was, so be it. He would have the truth from her today.

"Yes. I do love you."

"Then, what about the baby?" he demanded more vehemently. "If you claim to love me, why didn't you tell me you were carrying my child?"

Justine froze. "How did y—you—"

"The pills, Justine. Do you remember when I saw that bottle of vitamins while we were at the cabin in Alaska? The prescription was given by a Thomas Devane, M.D. When I returned to New York, I looked up the name in the phone book. He was no internist; the letters spelled out obstetrician. And there's one major reason a woman sees an obstetrician—and takes vitamins on prescription."

As he talked, Justine saw his anger mix with hurt. In her own shock at his awareness of her condition, she might have missed it, had it not been for the uncharacteristic luminescence of his dark, dark eyes.

Defensively, she turned, but he was close behind her with one fluid step. "Why didn't you tell me? It was my child, too. I had a right to know."

He had used the past tense; obviously he knew of her miscarriage. "You know I lost the baby?" she asked in a whisper, wrenched again by the loss.

"Yes. I had called the doctor to make sure you were well. I left my name and number with him. He was kind enough to call me when you miscarried." Again, she flinched, but Sloane was wrapped up in his own turmoil. "At least *he* agreed that I should know."

Justine whirled around to face the charge he made. His towering height, crowned with sparkling silver, nearly robbed her of breath. Gasping loudly, she caught herself.

"I couldn't tell you. You had asked me to marry you—I knew that you wanted marriage. I was frightened that—if you knew I was pregnant—you might use the child as a bargaining point. Don't you see? I was against marriage to begin with. And to enter into it—or be coerced into it—for the sake of a child would have been even worse!" Her voice had risen sharply. Now, she lowered it, recalling that particular time when she had discovered she was pregnant.

Avoiding his gaze, she forced herself onward, determined to tell the whole truth. "When I learned I was going to have a baby, we were only on businesslike terms. It was soon after you had manipulated my presence on your expedition. We weren't seeing each other in a personal way; I assumed it was over." Her eyes blurred at the thought; swallowing, she calmed herself enough to allow speech. "The baby became a substitute for you, Sloane. I couldn't have you. You wanted marriage or nothing, and I couldn't choose marriage. You have no idea how happy I was at the thought of having you—through your child—to live with always."

At that point, given the poignant truth she had just confessed, Justine knew that, if she hadn't reached Sloane yet, she never would. Her heart lurched when she looked up to see the lingering anger in his face. Cringing instinctively, she wrapped her arms about her and withdrew into herself. It was too late. There was no point in torturing herself further at the hand of his disdain. Turning to leave, his voice stopped her. Hurt had now superseded anger in his tone.

"You say you love me, yet you wouldn't share the joy of a growing child with me. What about Tony? You had no qualms about calling *him* to your bedside!"

An instant flashback to that evening in the hospital brought the blurred image of Sloane to her mind. At the time she had thought it her imagination. It seemed she was wrong. "So it *was* you at the door to my room. . . ?" she asked in soft wonder.

"That was quite a scene!" His nostrils flared, the grooves by his mouth deepened with his grimace. "One man comforting you on the loss of another man's child. . . !"

The first buds of hope sprung to life within her heart. If his hurt was spawned by jealousy, there was perhaps something to salvage after all. A tremulous smile toyed with her lips. "You were jealous," she stated in a soft whisper.

His answering boom shook her. "You're damned right I was jealous! And hurt. And angry. *I* should have been there with you, Justine. It was *my* child—*my* loss as well as yours. Not this fellow Tony—"

"You're wrong there, Sloane. Tony felt the loss deeply. That baby would have been a blood relative of his." At the mask of bewilderment that covered Sloane's face, she quickly explained. "Tony is my brother."

His retort was fast and sharp. "You said you had *no* siblings—"

"He's my *half* brother. He was born when I was six."

Bewilderment had turned to simple confusion as Sloane tried to put together the pieces of the jigsaw before him. "But, your parents were not divorced until you were nine. Tony was born . . . *before*?"

"Yes. The relationship between my parents was impossible. My father met and fell in love with another woman long before the divorce. That was one reason why it was so messy. Tony was born out of wedlock; my father married his mother when he was four."

For the first time there was genuine softening in Sloane's demeanor. "Did you know about . . . all this . . . when you were a child?"

She shook her head, sending ripples through the strawberry-blond curls which fell to her shoulders. "I met Tony for the first time when I was in college. He sought me out, on my father's instructions—though I didn't know that part until just recently. I never asked many questions of him; nor did he of me. We seemed to recognize a personal bond and clung to it as we became good friends. I knew nothing of his childhood until after the miscarriage . . . when we had it all out." She blushed. "He set me straight on a lot of things."

Sloane's attention was now fully hers. "Such as. . . ?"

This was the crux of her folly, the hardest part for her to accept. Pride swallowed, however, she forced herself to confess her ignorance. Wandering around his rigid figure, she approached the window, where the play of the evening lights of the city soothed her.

"Such as the fact that there was no love between my parents from the start," she began softly. "Such as the fact that theirs was simply a marriage of convenience gone wrong. Such as the fact that my father is a warm and caring man." Hesitating, she looked up. "I went to see him, Sloane."

"Your father?"

"Yes. I flew out to Montana last week. I felt it was something I had to do. I had to know the truth. Twenty-one years is a long time to live a misunderstanding. And if I hoped to start over with a clean slate . . ."

Her thoughts had been on her relationship with Sloane; his were still on her father. "What was his reaction to seeing you?"

Tears stung the backs of her eyes, but she refused to lower them. "He was ... stunned ... then thrilled. It was ... as though I'd given him the most precious gift . . ." Recalling her father's open show of emotion, one tear escaped at the corner of her eye. "We spent the week together, just getting to know one another. He is much as Tony said he was. I liked him." She paused for a deep breath. "And . . . I can believe that Tony did grow up in a home filled with love."

The air was quiet between them. Justine lowered her gaze to the floor. But there was more to her confession, words that could be held in no longer. "Tony said many of the same things you did, Sloane—that I've allowed my life to be shaped by misconceptions and misbeliefs—ideas that *I'd* chosen to accept as gospel. I've always prided myself on being right. Clear sighted. It's difficult to face the fact that I've been blinded all these years." She hung her head in humiliation, suddenly drained of spirit. It was Sloane's turn. If there was any future for them, he would have to help her now. Slowly, she turned and looked up at him. "I was wrong, Sloane. So wrong."

Above her was a face filled with similar sorrow and regret. Misinterpreting it, she began to tremble. But he raised his hands tentatively to her shoulders. His hold was light; its unsureness frightened her further.

"Your *brother*?" he whispered, shaking his head in disbelief. "*Damn!* I've been sick with jealousy! I thought you had lied to me— about other men in your life, about our love. I even thought . . ."— he faltered, his words tinged with self-reproach—". . . that the D and C was . . . that you . . . that you had wanted to . . ."

As the gist of his accusation hit home, Justine's tenuous composure snapped. Tears filled her eyes as she pulled away from him, shaking uncontrollably. "How *could* you think that? I *wanted* that baby! More than anything at the time, *I wanted that baby!*" Her sobs mingled with cries. "I *needed* that child, Sloane. If I couldn't have you, I needed *it!*" All sound was choked off as she wept against her hands. Her resistance was down when Sloane came to hold her, drawing her quivering body against him.

"We'll have another, sweetheart. We will. I promise you that."

It took several moments for his promise to reach her consciousness. Was the implication there? Did he still love her? Hands splayed against the firm warmth of his chest, she raised her tear-streaked face toward his. "Do you—can you—forgive me for my stupidity? For my stubbornness?"

The glow of love in his eyes, a sight she had seen before—in Westport, in Alaska—and cherished, surged into her with its heart-talk. "Love forgives all, Justine. And I love you. Never forget that." His lips lowered to touch hers, gently and sweetly, in slow reaquaintance. It was short but potent, a harbinger of all the fire to come. He was fully serious when he studied her face once more, searching and probing for the final solution.

"Once you believed that love, alone, was not enough," he reminded her. "What has made you change your mind?"

Unbidden, her hands crept up the sturdiness of his chest to his neck, then into the sterling shock of hair above and behind either ear. The surging joy within gave her strength, even as it brought tears of remembered agony to her eyes. She cried openly and without shame, knowing now that she could be her true self with Sloane. All was shared; there were no more secrets.

"I can't . . . live *without* . . . you, Sloane! I tried . . . but I can't. I need you . . . I'll always need you."

With a deep moan at the back of his throat, Sloane crushed her to him, embracing her with a fierceness totally removed from the earlier tentative hold. She was his, wholly and forever; as he hugged her, her love escaped its bounds and exploded into full glory. His words, spoken tenderly by her ear, thrilled her.

"I never thought to hear you say that. It took you so long, so terribly long to discover what I knew from that day we first made love. God, I love you, Justine! I love you!"

For long, quiet moments, they stood, wrapped in each other's arms, savoring the ecstasy that was now theirs. Kisses, touches, caresses were all secondary to the need to simply be close, to hold one another. It was Justine who finally broke the silence. Her eye held a ghost of humor, her lips the start of a smile.

"Did you really know it . . . way back then? You barely knew me then."

"I knew enough. And I've seen enough in life to know when I've finally found the real thing."

"You're just older and wiser," she ribbed him, fast growing high on his nearness.

Beneath her arms and hands, she felt the gradual relaxation of his body. He, too, was playful, almost giddy. "Not quite over the hill, my vixen," he growled, scooping her up in his arms and carrying her in the opposite direction toward what she assumed to be his bedroom.

"Put me down, Sloane," she giggled, offering token protest to his abduction.

"Never! You're mine, now. All mine."

She was given no time to examine the room he brought her to, for, no sooner had her back hit the yielding bedcovers, than he came down on top of her, blocking out all but the virile strength, the breathtaking beauty of his manhood. His kisses were more fevered, his touch more demanding. Waves of excitement broke within her, as his fingers fondled her, making short shrift of her silk blouse, then possessing the creamy fullness of her upthrust breasts. His tongue teased a rosy peak, coaxing it with little effort to hardness. In the riot of sensation which surged within her, she fought at the buttons of his shirt, finally laying his own chest open for her play. Her fingers caught in the fine dark hair, courting his flat nipple in passing, then delighting in his sharp intake of breath.

"Fair is fair," she chuckled softly, then gasped as his hand searched further, releasing her slacks and finding the warm, sweet core which craved his fullness. As though on mutual nod, each tore at his and her own clothes, satisfied temporarily to be flesh against flesh—until even that satisfaction vanished into a far greater need.

At that point, the telephone rang.

"I don't believe it!" Sloane exclaimed huskily. "I don't believe it!" Undaunted by the interruption, Justine continued her joy-play while her lover reached for the phone.

"Hello!" he barked darkly into the receiver. "What is it, Chad. . . ?" Her hand traced the line of dark hair across his chest, then down with tapered directness to the point of no return. Sloane's breathing quickened. "He wants . . . to meet . . . with us . . . now?" His eyes were on Justine, savoring the pleasure she received at the sight and feel of his body.

"You can't go now!" she cried, as he quickly muffled the phone.

His retort was hoarse. "Why not?"

Her hand had found what it sought and now caressed and fondled with devastating effect on Sloane. "I need you," she whispered seductively, moving closer to welcome him back.

His words were silent, only mouthed, and she caught every one. "Show me."

Her lips found the most sensitive places on his lean man's body and did just that, while Sloane struggled to cope with the telephone in his hand. "Sorry, Chad"—he cleared his throat futilely—"but either *you* meet with him . . ."—he tensed, then moaned, covering the phone to pant a hoarse-whispered "God, Justine!" before coughing a pretense of calm into his voice—". . . or . . . he'll have to wait . . . until tomorrow . . . What. . . ? Yes"—he looked pointedly at her, eyes growing more devilish by the minute—"I'm fine. Handle it . . . for me, Chad . . . will you. . . ? Thanks."

The phone was no sooner hung up than he lunged, pinning her beneath him on her back. "That was quite some trick! How cruel can you be?"

Her broad grin dimpled her cheeks. "You asked for it, lover. 'Show me.' Well, I tried!"

"You did ve—ry well, sweetheart. Now, let's take it from the top. We have a lot of making up to do!"

Making up they did, and then some. When they finally rested together, she knew the most complete sense of fulfillment she'd ever known. This present fulfillment had a past and a future from which it derived even greater enrichment.

Much, much later, with her hands wound around his muscled torso stretched lean and long beside her, she looked up at him. Her face bore the flush of passion, her eyes the emerald brilliance of love. "You *do* believe it will work, don't you, Sloane?"

She had never before seen such utter confidence on his face. "I *know* it will. Don't you know anything about the fox?" His enjoyment of her stunned expression was tempered by the profound implication of his words. "He mates only once, and then for life. Will you share my lair, Justine?"

Darkness permeated the room as she rolled over in the large bed and groped blindly for him. The emptiness beneath her hand alarmed her. "Sloane?" she called softly, then raised her voice. "Sloane?" With a smooth sweep, the covers fell back and she staggered from the bed, half-asleep, toward the closed door of the bedroom. Just as she reached it, it opened quickly, knocking her backward, throwing her off a balance which only Sloane's strong hands restored.

"Are you all right?" he asked in alarm, drawing her into the warm haven of his arms, kissing the pale copper crown of her head.

"I'm fine. Up to my old calamities. But I was worried. Where were you? I didn't hear any noise . . ."

"Another fact about the fox, my dear," he crooned, holding her to his side as he moved toward the bed, "is that he shares the duties of raising the young with his mate."

"The baby? Did he wake up?" Her arms slid around the solid column of her husband's neck. In an endearingly comfortable move, he lifted her into his arms, covered the few remaining feet to the bed, then laid her gently down.

"All fed and changed." He grinned in self-satisfaction. "And soundly back to sleep."

Her eyes glowed, even in the darkness, "You're a wonder, Sloane! And you've got to go to work tomorrow!"

"So do you, sweetheart." Pride surged within him as he visually devoured the graceful curves of his wife's body.

"Only part-time, though—"

"You need your rest, anyway. After all, you also have to contend with me and my son after hours. That's quite an undertaking."

Justine snuggled happily against him. "I love you!" she sighed in pure delight, breathing in the musky smell of him as though it were her sustenance.

Sloane angled up to better study her features, dim-lit by the night-light in the hall. "Are you sure? It's been almost two years. Are you still sure?"

"More sure than ever!" she replied, free of all doubt, all hesitancy, all fear.

Smiling in triumph, she burrowed more deeply against her love, her life, her soul mate. The Silver Fox may have stolen her heart, but he had given his own in return. No vixen could ask for more.

ABOUT THE AUTHOR

Barbara Delinsky is the author of more than twenty-three *New York Times*–bestselling novels including *Blueprints* and *Sweet Salt Air*. Her books have been published in thirty languages, with more than thirty-five million copies in print worldwide. A lifelong New Englander, Delinsky currently lives in Massachusetts with her husband.

BARBARA DELINKSY

FROM OPEN ROAD MEDIA

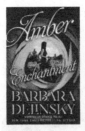

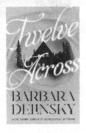